BILL DOYLE

CRIME THROUGH TIME ™

SWINDLED!

THE 1906 JOURNAL OF FITZ MORGAN

LITTLE, BROWN AND COMPANY

New York ✦ Boston

This book is dedicated to Alex Podeszwa
for being such an amazing kid.

–B.D.

Cover illustration by Steve Cieslawski
Back cover and interior illustrations by Brian Dow
Photos: pp. 4, 34, 44/Ablestock; pp. 7, 11, 80/Library of Congress
The Inspector photos: Library of Congress

Text copyright © 2006 by Bill Doyle
Compilation, illustrations, and photographs copyright © 2006 by Nancy Hall, Inc.
Crime Through Time is a trademark of Nancy Hall, Inc.
Developed by Nancy Hall, Inc.

Little, Brown and Company

Hachette Book Group USA
1271 Avenue of the Americas, New York, NY 10020
Visit our Web site at www.lb-kids.com

First Edition: March 2006

The characters and events portrayed in this book are fictitious. Any similarity to real persons, living or dead, is coincidental and not intended by the author.

Library of Congress Cataloging-in-Publication Data

Doyle, Bill H., 1968-
  Swindled! 1906 : the journal of Fitz Morgan / by Bill Doyle.— 1st ed.
    p. cm. — (Crime through time)
  Summary: On board the Continental Express, traveling from New York to San Francisco in 1906, fourteen-year-old amateur detective Fitz and a new friend, Justine Pinkerton, try to unravel a dangerous plot involving disguises, arsenic poisoning, and counterfeit money.
  ISBN 0-316-05736-3 (trade pbk.)
  [1. Railroads—Trains—Fiction. 2. Mistaken identity—Fiction. 3. Arsenic—Fiction. 4. Counterfeits and counterfeiting—Fiction. 5. Mystery and detective stories.] I. Title. II. Series: Doyle, Bill H. 1968- Crime through time.
PZ7.D7725Swi 2006
[Fic]—dc22   2005018598

10 9 8 7 6 5 4 3 2

Printed in the United States of America

ACKNOWLEDGMENTS

A thank-you of historic proportions to Nancy Hall for making this book and the Crime Through Time series a reality. To Kirsten Hall, for her keen editing and insightful grasp of the overall picture, and to Atif Toor for making the whole book come alive visually.

Special thanks to the editors at Little, Brown: Andrea Spooner, Jennifer Hunt, and Phoebe Sorkin, who are always dead-on, always incisive, and never discouraging. And thanks to Riccardo Salmona for his constant support.

New York City

California,
here I come!

CONTINENTAL EXPRESS
TRAIN EXCURSION TICKET

NEW YORK CITY
to
SAN FRANCISCO

one seat

Departure Date: *April 13, 1906*

HOLD THIS TICKET RECEIPT

April 13, 1906

The adventure of a lifetime has begun!

The night landscape of the eastern United States is whizzing by outside my window. I'm on board the Continental Express, a train bound from New York City to San Francisco. We're racing along the rails at thirty miles per hour, so this trip will take only five days. Just a few years back, it would have meant six months on a horse-drawn stagecoach. I would have been fifteen by the time we reached California!

Two hours ago Cousin Frederick dropped me off at New York City's Pennsylvania Station. What a madhouse! Whistles shrieked as trains clattered up to platforms. Shouting vendors wheeled their carts of fresh flowers and cured meats through the crowds of travelers. Choking clouds of smoke poured from the enormous black locomotives and hovered over the crowds. **I loved it!**

Penn Station—what a madhouse!

While people pushed by us at the entrance to the station, Cousin Frederick handed me a bag of cured-ham sandwiches and said, "Fitz, you tell that Aunt Elizabeth of yours hullo for me."

He gave my appearance one last disapproving look from under his bushy eyebrows. "You're full of grit, but don't go waking snakes on your vacation. Your father couldn't bear it if something happened to you, too."

Cousin Frederick

Frederick was talking about my family's bad luck. The flu had carried Mother away eleven years ago. And my brother, Killian, died three years later, in 1898. After that, Father and I were left knocking around in our big townhouse alone, and Father grew more and more protective of me. So much so that he waited until after my fourteenth birthday to let me visit Aunt Elizabeth in San Francisco.

I promised Cousin Frederick that Teddy and I would steer clear of trouble. Frederick looked a little doubtful, but with a quick wave he disappeared into the crowd, off to deliver blocks of ice from his horse-drawn cart.

Then I was alone with Teddy. Bundled up in a blue blanket, he squirmed in my arms. I cooed to him, "There, there, that's a good baby," loud enough for others to hear. I slid through the crowd to the ticket window—and my first challenge of the day.

"Where to, son?" the silver-haired ticket seller asked gruffly. Mystery and adventure! I wanted to shout. But remembering to keep my voice low, I answered, "San Francisco, please."

The ticket seller yawned (how could he yawn upon hearing such an exciting destination!) and pointed a finger at the swaddled bundle in my arms. "How old is the little one?"

"Just a pup," I replied, looking the man in the eye. Always maintain eye contact when working a case! It inspires trust in others.

Sleepy ticket seller

"Infants ride free." The ticket seller took my coins and slid my ticket through the window. He shouted, "Next!" to the person behind me when I didn't move along instantly.

Dizzy, I focused on the arrow pointing to my platform. I left the main terminal and plunged into the station's maze of tunnels. I didn't want to get lost and miss my train—which, according to the big station clock, was scheduled to leave in just nine minutes!

I shifted the bundle in my arms—which was getting heavy!—and out popped Teddy's tail, wagging happily. I couldn't help laughing. The detective training mission for today—pretending to carry a baby—was complete. I unwrapped Teddy from the small blanket and put him down.

President Teddy Roosevelt. My Teddy's namesake!

7

Teddy!

A frazzled businessman hurrying by did a double take as the "baby" gave his furry body a good shake, scratched behind his ears, and slobbered his tongue all over my outstretched hand.

I thought about telling the man, "Don't worry, sir, this bulldog is part of my training!" But even if he had not rushed off to catch a train, I doubted he would have understood. Not many people do.

Take my teacher Mrs. Kerrit. She definitely wouldn't understand. Six years ago, when I was eight, Mrs. Kerrit asked our class to list three things we wanted to be when we grew up. My friends put things like wife, king, or banker on their lists. I wrote:

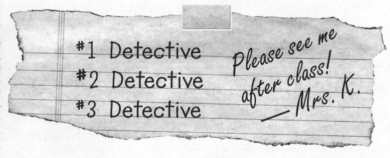

#1 Detective
#2 Detective
#3 Detective

Please see me after class!
— Mrs. K.

Mrs. Kerrit sent a note to Father, calling him in for a conference. She said that it was unrealistic for me to think I could ever be a detective like he is. Luckily, I've got a great father. He told her that it was possible. "Anything that's not worth fighting for isn't worth doing," he said.

Together we decided I might need to work harder than some other people, but I could sharpen my skills with a daily regimen of detective training—my version of a one-person investigator academy.

Now Teddy was yanking on his leash. I flicked my index finger three times toward the floor. This was one of the 25 or so silent commands Teddy and I had developed. Father jokingly called them "Teddyspeak." We had signals for "Open the door" (which Teddy could do by using his front paws while standing on his hind legs) and "Find Father's glasses."

The command I had just made meant "Wait a minute, Teddy," and my dog grudgingly sat down on the floor.

Before moving on, I wanted to get a quick look at my reflection in the nearby glass display case, just to make sure that I looked right. I did. My dark cap, which all the boys wear, sat straight on my head and hid most of my brown hair. I had on a grass-colored jacket—it covered my white shirt and suspenders—and matching knickers that ended at my knees.

Me—right now!

Teddy pulled on his leash again. He was right—we were running late. Time to get moving!

At the end of the corridor, we reached the platform next to our train—with just two minutes to spare! Steam

MY RULES OF DISGUISE

1) Keep it simple! Remember you want to blend in with your surroundings, not stand out with an odd-looking hat or mustache.

2) Create a story (including first and last name, age, birthplace, etc.) about your "new self" that you can tell others if they ask.

3) Be sure to carry "pocket litter" and other props in your pockets or bags. You might never carry ticket stubs or store receipts, but your "new self" might.

4) Study local accents and jargon so the way you talk doesn't betray you.

5) Never panic! Maintain eye contact, keep your voice steady, and stick with your story, even if you think you are about to have your identity revealed.

hissed from the locomotive as if the engine was begging to start racing down the rails. The cars behind the locomotive stretched the length of at least two football fields.

A mass of travelers, baggage handlers, screaming children, vendors' carts, skittish horses, and shouting porters swarmed between the passenger cars and us. "Stay close," I told Teddy by patting my hip twice.

"Watch out!" A thin woman pushing a baby carriage suddenly screamed, her voice rising above the din in panic.

With its horn blaring, a long black automobile came barreling through a gate meant for emergencies. It drove directly onto the platform, sending people scurrying in all directions. It screeched to a halt and just narrowly

My train!

missed the back wheel of the screaming woman's baby carriage.

The driver sprang from his seat and opened the back passenger door. I watched as a beautiful woman gracefully emerged. Most women wear their hair up these days, but her black hair ran down her back, nearly to her waist. Long black gloves covered her hands and extended up past her elbows.

WHY LEAVE YOUR PALACE?

Take it with you!

George Pullman built the first modern sleeping car in 1863. Later, he started the Pullman Palace Car Company. He wanted to give travelers a more comfortable way to travel—and he succeeded! Discover all the ways *your* Pullman car can transport you to luxury!

As the woman was handing the driver some money, a little girl who looked about six sprang out of the back of the car. The girl wore an expensive gray dress with ruffled petticoats, bloomers, and stockings. She had two pigtails tied tightly with ribbon the bright red color of

How most women wear their hair these days

The beautiful woman from the car

Grape belly wash

blood. The instant her feet hit the ground, the girl broke into a sprint, heading for a vendor's cart. Something—maybe the grape belly wash or another soft drink— must have caught her eye.

The woman took the girl's arm and gently pulled her back. Bending down, she whispered in the girl's ear, pointing across the platform. They both grew very still as they continued to stare.

I followed their gaze and discovered they were studying another little girl. She was pretty, with straight blonde hair that was swept up behind her head in a loose bun. She looked about nine years old, but she wore the long brown dress of someone much older—a woman who is serious and has an important job to do. No petticoats or ruffles for her, just straight lines. Only a bright purple scarf provided a splash of color.

The blonde girl was struggling to free her hand from the extremely large woman who stood next to her. The woman looked like a schoolteacher and held tight to the squirming girl's hand.

As a detective, I wanted to discover what made this girl special enough to attract stares. I moved a little closer to them and was just in time to hear the girl demand, "Why do you insist on holding my hand in public? It's humiliating! You are my governess, not my jailor!"

The woman took a deep breath, as if they had this argument all the time. "Until you are safely in the custody of the Pullman car porter, I cannot trust that you will not follow your whims. You know how you get distracted."

"I'll be the judge of that," the girl proclaimed. "Besides, I get focused. Not distracted."

The governess sniffed.

A tall man dressed in a porter's black uniform bounded up to them. About nineteen, he was skinny, all arms and legs. Before speaking he removed a shiny gold pocket watch from his vest pocket, flipped open the cover, and gave it a quick glance. He snapped it shut and looked at the girl and her governess.

"Hello! Right on time, I see. That's something I really admire," he said to the pair. "My name's William Henry Moorie. I'll be your porter for the trip to San Francisco."

The governess turned to him, pointed to the girl, and—to my amazement—said, "May I present Miss Justine Pinkerton."

I was thunderstruck! No wonder people were staring. The little girl was a Pinkerton. An actual Pinkerton!

The governess gave Justine's head a farewell pat and put the girl's hand into William Henry's. "She is all yours. Good luck. You are going to need it."

Justine instantly began defending herself to the porter. "My governess is exaggerating! She's just upset because she had to be rushed to the hospital once when—" I didn't hear any more because they disappeared into the crowd.

Justine Pinkerton

Suddenly, Teddy started barking at something in the air. What was the matter? I looked up. A fluttering green paper was floating by over our heads. I reached up, snatched it out of the air, and gazed at it in wonder.

A dollar bill.

Oh, the things I could buy—a magnifying glass,

Justine is a relative of "The Eye!"

INVESTIGATOR DAILY, July 2, 1884

FAREWELL TO OUR "FINDING" FATHER!

Allan Pinkerton died yesterday from a gangrenous tongue. He bit down on it during a fall on a Chicago street, and the cut later became infected. However, that is not the way we will remember the man whom many referred to as "The Eye." Allan Pinkerton was a Scottish immigrant and Chicago's first police detective. In 1850, he started The Pinkerton National Detective Agency, our country's first nationwide investigative company. Known by its trademark open eye and slogan "We Never Sleep," this agency has nabbed criminal after criminal and may have foiled an assassination plot against Lincoln in 1861. One of the company's specialties is railroad security.

fingerprint powder, the latest guide to blood typing. But, of course, these were just dreams. I had to return the bill to its rightful owner. I sighed. Sometimes it's not such fun to be one of the good guys.

I gauged the direction from which the bill had come and retraced its path. I figured it must have come from the back of the train, where a special Pullman car was hitched.

Most impressive

The car shone with the Great Seal of the United States. The car belonged to the government!

I spotted two men stepping from the shadows of the platform onto the Pullman car. They were too far away to see clearly.

"Hello!" I shouted, but they couldn't hear me. I headed toward them and lowered the pitch of my voice: "You dropped your dollar—"

"All aboard!" a conductor shouted. A sudden wave of passengers cut off my path as they shoved their way toward the train. I struggled against the tide of people but made no headway toward the two men.

It was no use. I gave up, put the dollar in my jacket pocket, and let the crowd push me toward the center of the train. Teddy and I climbed aboard the passenger car. Moments later the conductors blew their tin whistles, and the train pulled out of Pennsylvania Station.

I looked out the window of the passenger car door as the train—and the beating of my heart—picked up speed. I was on my way to San Francisco! The sun was setting, but I felt as if the curtain was rising on a great adventure.

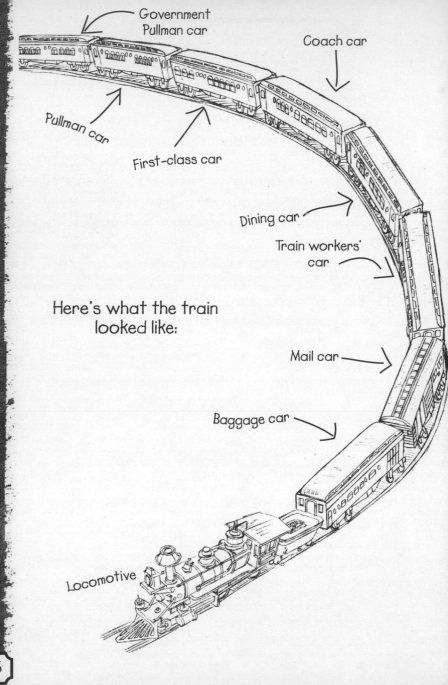

Government
Pullman car

Coach car

Pullman car

First-class car

Dining car

Train workers'
car

Here's what the train
looked like:

Mail car

Baggage car

Locomotive

6:30 AM

"Wake up! Wake up!"

The words dragged me out of sleep this morning and started my first full day on board the Continental Express.

I had figured the uncomfortable wooden bench and my excitement would keep me awake. But sometime during the night, the rocking motion of the train had lulled me into deep, dreamless sleep. Now I didn't want to wake up.

"Get up and play with me! Now! Now! NOW!" the voice whined.

I kept my eyes shut, pretending to be asleep. Silence. Whoever it is has left, I thought.

Then pop! Something wet sprayed all over my face.

What on earth? I opened one eye. Squinting against the light of the just-risen sun, I could make out a little girl with pigtails tied with blood-red ribbon. She was leaning against the seat in front of me and blowing bubbles of spearmint gum in my face.

Disgusting!

It was the girl from the platform who had arrived in the long black car. I closed my eyes and wondered why I'd never trained Teddy to bite pigtailed girls.

How rude!

The girl didn't leave. Instead, she became more insistent. "You're awake, silly boy. Don't pretend. Play a game of hide-and-seek. Now. In the baggage car. I really, really, REALLY want to!"

She paused, and I was sure she was getting ready to blow another saliva-filled bubble. My eyes flew open and I sat up, startling her. "Little girls shouldn't blow bubbles in the faces of strangers on trains," I said sternly.

Her lips puckered and she sucked in a long breath. I didn't need to be a detective to know I was about to witness the biggest tantrum in the history of the world. "What's your name?" I asked quickly, trying to avert the approaching storm of emotion.

The question took the wind out of her sails for a moment. "Asyla," she snuffled quietly. "Asyla Notabe."

Before I could introduce myself, Teddy growled softly, and a shadow fell over my seat. It was the woman with the long black hair and gloves. Looming over us, she said, "And I am Mrs. Rabella Notabe, her mother. Why are you bothering my daughter?" Her eyes flashed with anger.

Mrs. Rabella Notabe

I started to explain. "I—"

But Mrs. Notabe wasn't interested in what I had to say. She took her daughter's hand and they left. I could hear Asyla's whining drifting away as they headed out of the car.

Still in my seat, I stretched my stiff muscles and glanced around. The coach car was like a large open room, filled with 30 wooden benches just like mine. Almost all of the other seats were filled by families or businessmen.

An old-fashioned kerosene light

This old car was in pretty good shape but starting to fray around the edges. Windows—a few with cracks—lined each side and presented dusty views of the passing scenery. There were old-fashioned kerosene lights instead of gas, and they smelled like burning toast. Still, last night, those lamps had cast a dim but friendly glow as passengers had arranged themselves for the long trip.

Just then my stomach grumbled, letting me know it was time for breakfast.

"Hungry, Teddy?" I asked my bulldog, and almost instantly answered my own question. No! The sandwich bag that Cousin Frederick had packed was in tatters at my feet. Teddy had found it and eaten every last sandwich sometime in the night. There was no more food. Teddy looked up at me with his sad eyes, and I was just about to forgive him when he licked one or two last crumbs from his slobbering mouth.

So far it had not been the best start to the day.

Father had given me money for emergencies, and I had tucked it safely into my left sock. But since I was just hours into the trip, I didn't want to start spending it already.

Then I remembered I still had the dollar I found. And a dollar can buy a three-course breakfast in the dining car. I thought, I'll ask the men in the government Pullman if they lost a dollar yesterday on the platform. If they say they don't know what I'm talking about, I'll keep the dollar. Fair is fair.

"Stay!" I told Teddy, but I saw there was no need. His belly bulging, my bulldog was fast asleep, snoring happily.

Swaying with the rocking train, I walked toward the back of my car. I passed sleeping passengers and others who were enjoying breakfast: delicious smelling meats and bread they had packed (and which bad dogs had not eaten).

A menu from the dining car!

Continental Express

BREAKFAST

Fried Mutton Chops

✻

Fried Eggs

✻

Toast and Jam

✻

Tea and Coffee

The next car back was first class. Here travelers had much more comfort and privacy than in coach. Doorways that led to small compartments lined the hallway that ran the length of the car. Each of these compartments had two padded benches that faced each other—with plenty of room for the passengers inside to stretch out and enjoy meals brought by a porter.

I slid open the rear door of the first-class car and stepped out onto the connecting platform. A coupler joined this car to the Pullman behind it. The area between the two cars was open, and the rushing wind plucked at my cap and threw bits of dirt in my eyes. When I finally cleaned my eyes, I saw a small plaque to one side of the car's door:

"WE NEVER SLEEP-ER CAR"
PINKERTON PULLMAN

PRIVATE

NO TRESPASSING
AUTHORIZED PERSONS ONLY

If anyone is authorized, I am, I thought. I was on important business. I had a financial transaction to conduct with the government! Besides, I had to go through the Pinkerton car. It was the only way to get to the government Pullman, which was in back of this car.

I opened the hallway door and stepped inside. Luckily for me, a 30-foot-long hallway ran along one side of the Pinkerton car all the way to the other end. It let people pass through the car without disturbing the famous family of detectives. The Pinkertons' private quarters were on the other side of the hallway wall. They could be accessed only through locked doors at either end of the car. Thick red velvet curtains were drawn across the windows that ran along the outer wall, blocking out most of the early morning sun. Two electric bulbs burned in the middle of the hallway, spreading pools of dim light across the thick red carpet that ran the length of the passageway.

I closed the door behind me—and then froze.

When Killian was still alive, Father would take us fishing. After sitting in the hot sun all day, we'd want to take a dip in the water. Father would always say, "Never dive into unknown waters!" He had meant that the water might be shallower than you thought or you might bang into a submerged rock. But I think that warning works for every situation. Examining a new environment can be important in detective work. You never know what you might discover if you look before you leap.

Never dive into unknown waters!

My father

So I waited for my eyes to adjust to the dim light in the hallway. And my patience paid off.

Stretching across the floor, about three inches off the ground, was a thread. It was the color of the carpet beneath it— so it would be hard to see.

I crept closer and saw the thread was made of a very thin fiber. Someone passing through the hallway would snap it easily and wouldn't even know it. But the broken thread would show that an "intruder" had been there.

I had the feeling I knew who had stretched the thread across the hall—Justine Pinkerton.

So, I thought, Justine thinks she's a detective, does she? Well, let's see if her skills match mine. This would be an

Someone else must have seen this ad from THE INSPECTOR

excellent opportunity for me to get in a little detective training and keep my skills sharp.

I started to lift my foot over the thread. Then I stopped. I asked myself: What would I do if I wanted to catch even the cleverest observer?

I answered: I would tie two pieces of thread across the hall, not just one.

With this in mind, I inspected the area near the first thread more closely. Aha! There it was—another thread. This one was several inches from the first, but tied at chest level.

I squeezed between the two threads and breathed a sigh of relief. I walked to the end of the hallway, feeling sure that I had been able to bypass the security devices without triggering either of them.

When I stepped out onto another connecting platform, the wind slammed into me again, and the clacking of the train was deafening.

In front of me loomed the government Pullman with the Great Seal of the United States emblazoned on the door. Eager to get off the windy, noisy platform, I raised my hand to knock.

The door flew open—and a man staggered out! He was a huge man with a sweating face and a giant handlebar mustache. His eyes were blank and rolled about in their sockets. His arms waved as if he were playing a game of blindman's buff.

But this was no game.

Without warning, he lunged at me.

"Stop!" I cried above the roar of the wind. But he didn't seem to hear me. I leaped to the side and ducked as his meaty hands blindly swept the air over my head.

He took a step forward and teetered at the edge of the small platform. The sharp rocks along the tracks rushed by below like the teeth of a moving saw. One more step and he would tumble off the speeding train!

Yikes!

His right foot lifted and he started to sway. I grabbed for him—and missed! He was going over!

I tried again—this time catching onto a loose piece of his jacket.

Got you! I thought. But the large man's forward momentum was too strong. I couldn't slow his progress. The weight of his body dragged me toward the edge—and I realized we were both going to fall over the side!

For one horrid instant we each had a foot dangling off the train. Cinders from the locomotive burned my skin and singed my hair.

Suddenly, my free hand latched onto the brass handrail bolted to the Pullman.

With one hand on the rail and another grasping the man, I used our forward motion to swing us back, as if we were the pendulum of a clock. I screamed with the strain and swung the man onto the train. The force sent him banging into the wall of his car, and he slid limply to the floor.

Before I could move away from the edge of the platform, the train screeched over a bit of loose track, and the cars lurched to the side. My arms were pin-wheeling, searching for something—anything!—to grab onto . . . but my fingers couldn't find the handrail. I was heading straight over the side!

Lightning fast, a hand shot out, grabbed my flailing hand, and jammed it against the rail. I grabbed on with all my remaining strength, pulling myself back onto the platform with such force that I stumbled and landed flat on my back.

I was safe.

Out of breath and shaking, I looked up to see who had saved me. It was Justine Pinkerton! She was leaning over me, grinning, with her hand cradling the back of my head so it did not bang on the hard surface of the train.

"Bully for you! You saved the man's life," she shouted above the wind.

"And you saved mine. Thank you!" I stood up, quickly tucking loose hairs under my cap. "He's unconscious. We'd better get him inside."

Justine reached inside the compartment and rang the electric button that would call the porter. Then she grabbed the man's legs. I hooked my hands under his armpits, and working together, we were able to drag him halfway through the door of the Pinkerton car.

"Gads, what's this man been eating? Rocks?" Justine asked when we set him down and paused to catch our breath. While most of his body remained on the connecting platform between the two cars, at least we had managed to get his head out of the elements.

"Do you know him?" I

She saved my life!

asked. When Justine shook her head, I reached into the man's jacket and took out a black leather wallet. Inside was a badge, and I gazed at it in awe. "Say hello to special agent Nathan Howard of the United States Secret Service," I told Justine Pinkerton.

SECRET SERVICE NOW HIRING!

Want a job with the Secret Service?
Here is what you should know about us:

1865 At the end of the Civil War as much as one half of all U.S. paper money in circulation was counterfeit! We were created to fight this problem.

1867 Our duties now included detecting anyone who commited fraud against the government. This led to investigating mail robbers, the Ku Klux Klan, smugglers, and many others!

1902 A year after the assassination of President McKinley—the third president killed in 36 years—we took full-time responsibility for protection of the president.

If you are ready for challenge, excitement, and danger—join us!

Who knows? Someday I might work for them!

"Secret Service!" Justine shouted in excitement. I knelt beside Agent Howard and gave him a good shake, but he didn't wake up.

William Henry, the porter

Just then the tall, skinny porter, William Henry, rushed into the hallway. He looked flustered. "Miss Pinkerton, you have to stop pressing that button—" William Henry stopped and his eyes widened in surprise when he spotted me. "What's he doing here?"

"Who?" Justine asked, as if she didn't understand what he was talking about. Then she said, "Oh, him. This is my friend. His name is . . . his name is . . . "

"Fitz," I said. "Fitz Morgan."

"Your family gave strict orders. There are to be no guests in this Pullman car," William Henry warned Justine.

"I'll be the judge of that," she replied.

William Henry was about to say something, when he finally noticed Agent Howard. "My stars!" he shouted. "There's a man on the floor!"

"Brilliant deduction," I said sarcastically, continuing my quick examination of Agent Howard. Lifting one of his hands, I felt a faint, rapid pulse. I also noticed that his fingernails were a bright cherry red. Quickly, I looked at his face—his lips were the same cherry red.

I leaned closer to his mouth and caught the faint whiff of bitter almonds on his shallow breath. Oh no! I thought.

"What happened here? Someone tell me this instant!" William Henry demanded.

"We aren't sure," Justine replied. "Maybe he fainted."

I looked at her. "No. He didn't faint," I said. "This man is in a coma. He's been poisoned!"

DETECTING POISON: CYANIDE CHECKLIST

Is a person showing some or all of the following symptoms?

- Sudden collapse or coma

- Skin, nails, and lips that are unusually pink or cherry red. This color is caused by the way cyanide blocks oxygen from getting into cells, so the oxygen remains in the blood

- Very fast breathing and either a very fast or very slow heartbeat

- Breath that smells like bitter almonds

I keep this list on me just in case!

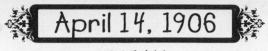
Together, the three of us carried Agent

Howard into the Pinkerton Pullman and laid him on a plush, green sofa.

While Justine placed a pillow under his head, William Henry took my arm. He smelled like soap, and his uniform was spotless, but I noticed his hands and fingernails were stained with grease. "Poisoned, you say?" he said doubtfully. "And what would a little boy know about poison?"

There was no time to go into my background with a fool.

"If I'm right, this man has been poisoned by cyanide."

William Henry gripped my arm harder and scoffed, "You're out of your mind!"

"Listen," I said. "Time is of the essence. This man has to get an injection of amyl nitrate quickly."

"Amyl nitrate? But that's a very dangerous chemical. It might kill him!"

I was surprised William Henry knew what amyl nitrate was.

"All the antidotes to cyanide are poisons. Once someone loses consciousness, he has to receive an antidote within the first half hour or he'll die," I said shaking my arm free of William Henry's grasp. "This man needs medical attention. And every second counts."

William Henry's bright blue eyes turned to Justine. "He's right," she told him. "You must get help now."

"Fine then. I'll go," William Henry said, heading to the door. "But I want you to wait in the laboratory until I get back—away from Agent Howard. With that, William Henry rushed to get help.

Surprised, I turned to Justine. "You have a laboratory?"

"Of course," Justine answered matter-of-factly. Opening an interior door, she gestured for me to follow her.

We left the living area with its gold fixtures and overstuffed furniture, and entered the sleeping area.

"There are four separate sleeping compartments here," Justine told me, pointing to each of the four doors as we walked down a small hallway. She didn't seem to be showing off, just stating a fact.

Suddenly she stopped, looked at me, and asked, "Do you really think someone poisoned Agent Howard? It'd be wrong to shout, 'How thrilling!' wouldn't it? Perhaps we should give him some of that new drug called aspirin. Have you heard about it?"

Then without waiting for an answer, she turned and opened another door. We entered the laboratory.

When I saw it, my eyes nearly popped out of my head. It took up about the same amount of space as my coach car, but that's where the similarities ended.

This laboratory had two electric fans, an electric heater, velvet armchairs, lighters for cigars—all beneath the most beautiful stained glass ceiling. But what impressed me most was that the Pullman was jammed with the most advanced criminal detection equipment in the world.

When I finally finished my survey of the room, I noticed that Justine was studying me.

She said, "I've seen that look before. You have detective work in your blood."

I felt my face flush—I didn't want her sharp eyes looking too closely at me. And, to tell the truth, I also felt a little jealous. Why should she have access to all this wonderful equipment? She probably didn't even know what half of it was!

Blood-typing tools   Microscope   Photographic equipment

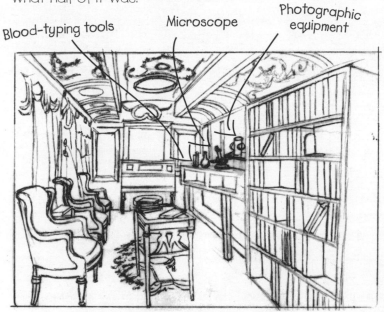

The Pinkertons' mobile laboratory.

I blurted out, "What does a little girl like you know about detective work?"

She just laughed, not seeming to mind my sharp tone. "You sound like William Henry! But to answer your question, I'm a Pinkerton. I've been surrounded by detectives my whole life. My father's one of them. In fact, he uses this car to solve crimes across the country."

I examined a modern microscope at the work desk and tried to keep from drooling. "You're allowed to travel alone?" I asked. I really meant, You're just a baby.

"Of course," she replied. "I'm wise beyond my years."

"What does that mean?"

She shrugged and said, "Everyone I meet says it—except my governess. She says she needs a break from me. That's why she stayed back in New York. My family lives there, but Mother and Father are in Sacramento now."

"Is your father working on a case?" I asked, as my eyes wandered to a framed note from the late President Abraham Lincoln. It thanked the Pinkertons for bringing many criminals to justice.

"My parents were returning from the Far East by way of California when my father got a telegram," Justine said. "He was needed in Sacramento to help solve a string of mysterious bank robberies. Father asked the train company to bring him our Pullman. I came along for the ride. Once we arrive in San Francisco, this car will be attached to another train that will take me up to Sacramento."

I was only half listening to her. Standing in front of a tall bookcase that took up an entire wall of the laboratory, I was running my eyes greedily over row

The Modern Microscope

This type of microscope incorporates more than lens so that the image m nified by one lens can be further magnified by ano

NOW AVAILABLE WITH SPECIA FEATURES

Something from my wish list!

after row of beautiful books. The leather bindings had titles such as CRIMINAL INVESTIGATION by Hans Gross, FINGERPRINTS by Sir Francis Galton—and hundreds of others. It was the most complete library of crime and detection I had ever seen!

Justine noticed my gaze and said, "I've read them all. Well, almost all. I love criminology. Don't laugh, but my dream is to be the first woman in my family to go to law school." As if to keep me from teasing her, she quickly continued, "These books helped me set up the hallway alarm you triggered—"

"I did not! I sidestepped all your devices," I cried, sounding more defensive than I'd intended. Justine just laughed again. "What alarm did I trigger?" I asked.

"I can't tell you that. I never know when that snoop Fitz Morgan might try to trespass again," she replied, her eyes gleaming happily. "You set off my alarm, and I came to investigate. It's a good thing, too. You need looking after."

Not by a spoiled girl like you, I almost said, but thought better of it. Envy was getting the better of me. Instead I told her, "I can take care of myself, thank you."

"I'll be the judge of that," Justine said once again. She jutted out her chin in a way she probably thought made her look tough. But to me it just looked funny. Now it was my turn to laugh.

"Don't you dare make fun of me," she shouted. "I forbid it!"

This only made me laugh harder and helped to push aside my bad feelings. After all, I thought, Justine was sharing her dreams with me—not to mention, she had saved my life! It was time I got over my jealousy and acted my age.

"I'll be the judge of that," I said, mimicking her and giving her a genuine smile.

She still looked a little hurt, so after a moment of thought, I added, "In fact, from now on, I think I'll call you Judge."

She shook her head. "That doesn't make sense. There aren't any female judges."

"Then calling yourself Judge Pinkerton will give you a head start in changing things."

She was silent for a moment, thinking it over. "Judge ... hmm ... I guess I could live with that." But it was clear from her happy expression that she really liked the name.

Just then we heard a door open in the other room. We rushed back to where Agent Howard lay motionless on the sofa in time to see William Henry enter with two men. He pointed to the shorter of the two and said, "This is Mr. Spike. He's the lead conductor and my boss."

Mr. Spike was a bald, round-faced man who wore a uniform similar to William Henry's. But this man's thick neck bulged over the sides of his collar.

Judge Pinkerton

"And"—William Henry gestured to a distinguished-looking man with a closely cropped white beard and perfectly round glasses—"may I present Dr. Sigmund Freud?"

I felt my heart leap. Dr. Freud! THE Dr. Sigmund Freud was standing two feet away from me!

Dr. Sigmund Freud

Austrian to Amaze at Lecture

Straight from Vienna, Dr. Sigmund Freud will give a lecture tonight on something he calls "psycho-analysis." Come hear Dr. Freud's strange new ideas about the unconscious mind, listen as he interprets dreams, and discover the origins of mental illness in childhood events! His talk promises to be quite exciting.

Los Angeles is the last stop on Dr. Freud's American lecture circuit. You will not want to miss this unique opportunity.

Masonic Hall, 7:00 PM.

Judge tore out this ad from a magazine for me

I started to explain quickly. "Dr. Freud, this man is a government agent. And he's been pois—"

But I was interrupted by Mr. Spike, who waved a finger in my face. "Children," he said in a syrupy voice, and from the very first syllable I knew that he was a talker-downer. Talker-downers can't stop themselves from talking down to every child they meet.

Mr. Spike said, "I've got a son myself, and so I know youngsters have a way of making far too much of things." I wanted to say that I felt sorry for his son, but didn't.

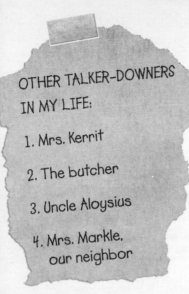

OTHER TALKER-DOWNERS
IN MY LIFE:

1. Mrs. Kerrit

2. The butcher

3. Uncle Aloysius

4. Mrs. Markle,
   our neighbor

"William Henry tells me you believe this man has been poisoned? That's just preposterous. And such talk, even from children, could cause panic on the train. We have a schedule to keep. This man probably just ate too much bacon at breakfast. Our job is to take care of him and his stomachache. Your job is to be good children."

This is insane! I thought. Agent Howard didn't have a "stomachache"!

"That's not—," I started to protest, but Mr. Spike cut me off again, this time by turning his back to me and addressing Judge.

"Miss Justine," he said coldly, "I'd hate to have to tell your parents that you are really not mature enough to ride this train by yourself."

I saw Judge's whole body tense at the threat, and she glared at Mr. Spike. But she kept her mouth closed. Seeing that he had silenced both Judge and me, Mr. Spike gave us an icy smile and left the compartment.

William Henry looked at us. "All right, you two," he said.

"You heard Mr. Spike. Into the laboratory compartment with you."

Seeing Dr. Freud remove a needle from his bag and turn toward Agent Howard, William Henry practically pushed us along.

Even though Judge and I were banished to the laboratory compartment, I felt better knowing that Agent Howard was in the capable hands of Dr. Freud. He would know what to do.

We were lucky that Dr. Freud was there!

Judge sighed. "It looks like we're going to miss all the fun."

I didn't agree. "We need to get a look at the scene of the crime."

"Agent Howard's Pullman. What a fantastic idea!" Judge cried. Then she grinned and said in a fake sugary voice, "But aren't you worried about Mr. Spike? He told us to be 'good little children.'"

"Yes, he did," I answered. "But I think the definition of 'good' is doing the right thing, and that means getting to the truth."

"I couldn't agree more," Judge said. "Let's go!"

We opened the door that led from the laboratory to the semi-public hallway. Suddenly Judge whispered, "Wait a second," and rushed back into the laboratory. She returned moments later carrying a small black case. "A kit for collecting evidence," she explained.

"Good thinking," I said and thought to myself that it looked like Justine was going to turn out to be a good investigative partner.

We were continuing down the hall when Judge suddenly stopped in her tracks. "Fitz, I guess you triggered more than one of my alarm systems after all." She was examining the two threads I had stepped between. Each one had been snapped in two.

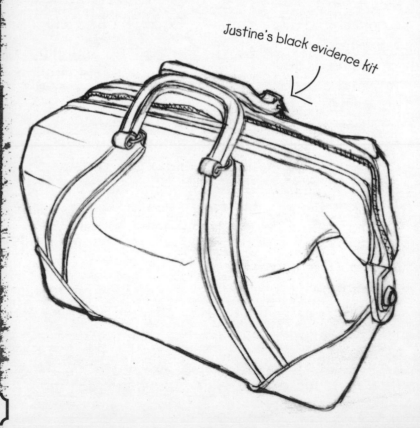

Justine's black evidence kit

"Nonsense," I protested. "You must have broken them when you rushed to help Agent Howard and me."

But Judge insisted that I had done it, so I changed the subject. "What alerted you that I was in the hall? How did I miss it?" I asked.

She chuckled. "I'll take that secret with me to the grave. Which, now that I think about it, I hope isn't anytime soon. What if the person who poisoned Agent Howard is still in the government car?"

"That would make him or her a fool," I said, "which means he or she wouldn't be much of a threat."

By now we were on the noisy platform outside the open door of the government Pullman. I knocked, and there was no answer.

"I hope you're right," Judge said.

With that, we stepped inside.

Can you believe
this office is on
a train?

We stepped through a kind of foyer

and found ourselves in a mobile office. The inner wall was lined with tall cabinets for documents and a bookcase holding paper and other supplies. Two dark wooden desks sat against the outer wall, facing large curtained windows. Papers were blowing around because of the wind from the open door.

My detective's eye found one thing especially noteworthy. There was a broken teacup on the desk closest to us. Its handle had snapped off, and the pieces lay on the wooden surface.

Definitely a clue!

I wanted to rush over to the desk and examine the broken cup. Patience, I told myself. Don't dive into unknown waters.

We looked around the compartment quickly, just to make sure that no one was hiding in the shadows. Then we got to work.

Removing a small pad of paper from my jacket pocket so I could take notes, I said, "It's wrong to make assumptions. But thanks to that teacup, I think we can safely assume this is where Agent Howard was poisoned. That makes this compartment the scene of the crime. And that means there's loads of evidence just begging to be discovered!"

I remembered that detectives move in patterns to ensure that every inch is studied when they walk through and inspect a crime scene. We started at the door of the compartment and circled inward toward the desk. We slowly went around and around, and I had to force myself not to skip ahead in my eagerness to spot a clue. We had to examine every object we came to, and that included even boring things such as a suitcase filled with mostly dirty clothes and a sports magazine from two months ago. I made myself look at each item carefully—the solutions to many crimes are hidden in the little details.

In one corner we found an old top hat and in another we discovered a fishing rod. "Interesting," Judge observed, holding up the rod. "Agent Howard must enjoy fishing as a hobby."

I was tempted to say, Interesting, perhaps, but not very helpful, but just then the lure at the end of the line caught my eye.

"My brother was a fisherman, and I don't think this is a real lure," I said.

"What do you mean?" Judge looked at the rod curiously.

I answered her question with a question: "Do you have anything metallic?"

This is a real lure

Why use bait wh
ur handy-dandy

Judge reached into her pocket, took out a metal key and held it out to me.

"Watch this." I held the lure over the key. The key shot from her hand and attached itself to the lure with a click. "This lure is a magnet!"

44

"A magnet? What exactly is Agent Howard fishing for?" Judge asked. "Tin fish? Metal mackerel?"

I had no answer, so I just put the rod back in the corner.

We continued on our circular path and finally reached the desk. This is where we'll uncover the real clues, I hoped.

It was finally time to examine the broken teacup! A pattern of dried liquid had expanded from the cup—as if the liquid had sprayed out when the cup had been dropped and broken.

Hmmm... had there been poison in the cup? Was the cup Agent Howard's?

A fingerprint might answer the second question.

Every detective knows that when people touch a surface, they leave behind a pattern of oil and sweat in the shape of their fingertip ridges. Because everyone's ridges are unique, everyone leaves behind a one-of-a-kind print.

"I need—" I started to say.

But Judge was already on the case. She had opened her evidence kit and taken out a small jar shaped like a spice shaker. "Fingerprint powder," she said.

"Do you have a soft brush and sticky slides in there?" I asked.

"Of course," Judge said. She was really starting to amaze me.

I examined the cup but was careful not to touch it. I didn't want to smudge any existing prints or add my own to the mix.

No fingerprints jumped out at me. But that didn't mean they weren't there. I knew that surfaces are usually covered in people's prints. To find them is just a matter of looking at things the right way—holding a light at a different angle or looking through a magnifying glass.

"I don't see anything," Judge said from over my shoulder. I nodded, and sprinkled fingerprint powder on the cup, hoping it would reveal at least one print.

I followed the steps my father had taught me to lift a fingerprint: Remember T.O.E.!

"There it is . . . " I breathed softly as I finally spotted a print.

"Yes!" Judge shouted, seeing what I meant.

Remember T.O.E.!

1) **T**ap some fingerprint powder lightly over the object or surface where you suspect you'll find a print.

2) **O**verlay the sticky side of the glass slide on the powder. (Use a light glue or adhesive to make the slide sticky.)

3) **E**ase the slide off the object or surface.

There were several other bits of prints on the cup, but the one I had lifted was a nice, clear one.

"Bully for you! It's gorgeous." Judge took the slide from me, handling it by its edge. She slipped it in a protective paper sleeve and put it into her collection kit.

"Now we just need a fingerprint from Agent Howard," I said. "That way we can compare the two. If his matches this one, we know he's the one who drank from this cup."

My nose began to tickle from the fingerprint powder. I raised my head to sneeze . . . and saw thin scratch marks on one end of the ceiling.

"Ah!" I cried and slapped my forehead. We had very carefully looked for clues on the floor and the walls, but we had forgotten to look up!

I pulled a chair over to stand on so I could get a better look at the marks. They started about four inches out from the wall and then disappeared into a small gap between the ceiling and the top of the wall.

"Do you think there's a space behind the wall?" Judge asked. That's exactly what I thought. "But if so," she asked, "how would someone retrieve what they hid there?"

I pondered this for a minute and then said, "Can you hand me the fishing rod?"

When she handed me the rod, I placed the lure inside the gap and let it fall. As I did, I noticed that the top of the rod added a thin scratch to the ceiling.

I let out line from the reel, and the lure made scuffling sounds like a mouse traveling down inside the wall. Finally, I heard a metallic click as the magnetic lure attracted something. Very slowly, as if I had an enormous salmon on the line, I reeled in the lure. Something banged against the wall as it rose higher and higher.

The box was tiny!

A small metal box appeared in the gap. It was about eleven inches wide but only two inches high— so it could fit through the hole.

Climbing off the chair, I handed the rod to Judge and set the box on the desk. We stared at it for a moment.

"We should open it," I said. My curiosity was like a

strong itch I needed to scratch. "It could contain a clue."

Judge shook her head. "It could also contain government secrets. Classified information."

"If it does, we'll put it back in the box and not tell anyone about it. I think we can be trusted with a few secrets—or would you rather give it to Mr. Spike?"

Just saying his name convinced her. There was no lock on the box, and the latch clicked open with a slight push.

Inside was a dark brown file with a label reading USS MAINE.

I felt my eyes filling with tears as I looked at the name USS MAINE. It had been eight years, but the memories still hurt.

"What is it?" Judge saw my reaction and her voice filled with concern. "What's wrong?"

OFFICIAL MEMORANDUM

DATE: February 12, 1904

SUBJECT: Destruction of USS Maine.

FINDINGS:

The battleship Maine exploded in the harbor of Havana, Cuba, on February 15, 1898. At that time, Spain was blamed for the explosion—and the sinking of the ship was the final straw that led to war between the United States and Spain.

Our investigations have shown that perhaps Spain was innocent, and that one of its mines was not the cause of the sinking. The explosion was probably caused by something inside the ship, perhaps combustion in the ship's coal bins.

↖ A page from the file we discovered

"I can't . . ."

"Here." Judge pushed a chair over for me, and I sat down.

"I just... It's so strange to see this... It was a long time ago." I fumbled for words but then collected myself. "My brother Killian was lost on the MAINE. I still carry his photograph."

Judge looked at the picture I had taken from my jacket pocket, and then put a hand on my shoulder. "Oh, I'm so sorry."

And I could see in her deep brown eyes that she was. Somehow this made me want to tell her more.

Killian

"After Killian was lost, things were never quite the same around our house. My father, he's a great man, don't get me wrong—but he didn't smile or laugh as much. We had a memorial service for Killian, but he went down with the MAINE so we didn't have a body.

I paused and wiped my teary eyes. "It all happened years ago. I'm being silly...."

"I'll be the judge of that," Judge said, smiling.

I smiled back. Taking the photograph of my brother, I looked at Killian's face and the large birthmark under his right eye that he used to say looked like a map of Asia. Then I turned away from the past and back to the case at hand.

Secret Service agents are in charge of protecting important people and investigating counterfeit cases. What did the MAINE have to do with the Secret Service? And what could it possibly have to do with Agent Howard being poisoned?

Nothing was the only answer I could think of. I put the file back in the box and, like returning a fish to the sea, I dropped this red herring back into the space behind the wall.

William Henry looked
peeved, all right!

April 14, 1906

5:30 PM

We were repacking Judge's evidence

kit when William Henry entered the Pullman. In his arms, he held a squirming, slobbering creature, which he pushed on me as if it were a soiled baby. "Why do I know this beast belongs to you? I found him sniffing around first class."

"Teddy!" Just who I needed to cheer me up. I took my bulldog from him, but rather than scolding Teddy for leaving our seat, I gave him a good scratch behind his ears.

William Henry frowned at us. "And I will not even name the thousands of reasons you should not be in this car."

"Good. What information do you have?" Judge asked as I put Teddy on the floor.

Glaring at me, William Henry said, "If you don't get out of this car now, you're going to get me in trouble. I'm responsible for Miss Pinkerton."

"Oh, come on, are you a man or a schoolmarm?" I said, and saw his eyes spark.

Judge added quickly, "William Henry, Mr. Spike is a fool. Somebody has to do something."

William Henry sighed, took off his cap, and ran a hand through his thick brown hair. "All right, but I am not helping you. I'm just passing along information."

"Understood," I said, but thought, *Oh, just tell us, you big baby!*

"We're scheduled to stop in Cincinnati in three hours,"

William Henry began. "But Dr. Freud believes the man, while still unconscious, is out of danger. The amyl nitrate has blocked the destructive power of the cyanide without killing him. Dr. Freud thinks he would be better off remaining on the train until San Francisco, where he can receive the best medical care."

If I'd had the time, I would have loved to have visited the Palace of Fans—Home of the Cincinnati Reds base-ball team!

Since William Henry seemed willing to share information, I asked, "Who else had access to this car?"

"This Pullman belongs to the government."

I said impatiently, "Yes, we know. But who else had access?"

"Well, I did. And Agent Howard, of course."

"And the other man?" I asked.

He blinked. "What other man?"

I scowled at him. "Yesterday, at Pennsylvania Station, I saw two men board this Pullman. In fact, they dropped a dollar bill, which I was trying to return to them this morning."

"You're full of balloon juice. I haven't seen anyone else in this car."

Balloon juice? Who did he think he was talking to? "That only means you haven't seen the other man," I hissed between clenched teeth. "It doesn't mean that he hasn't been here."

William Henry mouthed the words "balloon juice" to Judge and made a face as if indicating that I was crazy.

I felt my fingers curl into fists.

"But Agent Howard did have a cat!" Judge blurted, cutting through the tension. "I saw a man carrying a cat last night when he passed through our car to the dining car. The poor thing was very still and looked like it was sick. It must be frightened and is hiding, because I haven't seen it since."

What I imagine Judge saw last night

"Not to worry." I leaned down to pat Teddy, who had been sleeping at my feet. His big head rose groggily.

"Cat. Find cat, Teddy. Find cat," I said to him out loud. But Teddy just looked at me, wagging his tail. He was waiting for me to give him a hand signal in Teddyspeak. With my right hand I pointed sharply away from me, the signal for FIND.

He didn't budge. Find what? his eyes asked.

I glanced at William Henry, and wished he wasn't watching this. Then, I turned back to Teddy and made the signal for CAT. I stuck out my tongue and put two fingers behind my head like pointy ears.

William Henry burst out laughing and I felt my face redden, but it was worth it. Teddy understood the signal. He began to sniff around the room. Finding nothing that interested him, he propped himself on his hind legs and used his front paws to turn the brass doorknob. It took a few little hops to reach the knob, but when he got the door open, Teddy trotted off to check the rest of the train.

Teddy would love this!

HOUSE DETECTIVE: PAVLOV UNIVERSITY

BASIC CANINE DETECTION SKILLS 101

COURSE DESCRIPTION: In this class you will learn the secret of training your four-legged friend to crack your next case.

1) Practice with your dog in a room filled with different objects.

2) In a commanding voice, say, "Find ball," or whatever you want Fido to find.

3) When Fido gets near the ball, reward him with food. Congratulations. Fido knows what "ball" is.

4) Say, "Find ball," again. This time, wait for Fido to bring the ball to you and give him more food. Now Fido knows he should bring the ball you to get more treats.

William Henry chortled. "I believe I can die a happy man, for now I've seen everything. You might just as well have asked that old shoe to find the cat."

I had my doubts about Teddy—the smell of a piece of cheese would be enough to distract him from his mission. But I didn't want to give William Henry the satisfaction of knowing that. "Don't die yet. You'll want to see me crack this case first," I said coolly.

I wanted to show him he was dealing with a skilled detective, so I continued in my professional-sounding voice. "We should write down what we know so far. It will help us focus."

Taking a pen from the desk, I wrote:

What we know so far:

1. Agent Howard has been poisoned.
2. Two men boarded government Pullman. Only one has been seen since.
3. Suspect may still be on the train.
4. Agent's cat may be on the train.

The three of us looked at the list.

William Henry tapped the paper with one grease-stained finger. "There are 173 people on board this train. How can we determine who the criminal is?"

"Simple," I answered, talking off the top of my head. I wanted to regain some ground with William Henry, and so I tried to sound confident. "We narrow down that large number to a smaller number of suspects."

He arched a blonde eyebrow doubtfully. "Yes, but how?"

"We figure out what kind of people commit a crime like poisoning and make a description of their personality traits." I gained steam as I spoke. "Then we compare that description to the passenger list. Whoever doesn't match that description, we eliminate."

"That's brilliant!" Judge cried. "They did something similar in the Jack the Ripper case in London almost twenty years ago."

"Exactly," I said. "We have to create a criminal profile! Let's go back to the laboratory compartment and begin."

Once there, we settled onto the comfortable chairs

LONDON TIMES, 1889

WHO IS JACK THE RIPPER?

George B. Phillips, a police surgeon in London, England, was the first person to make a personality profile in an attempt to catch a criminal. Dr. Phillips was trying to catch none other than Jack the Ripper, the killer who murdered seven women in London in 1888. After looking at the wounds of the third victim, Dr. Phillips determined that the killer must have a medical background.

Later, police surgeon Thomas Bond contradicted this profile. He examined the last victim of Jack the Ripper and said, "In each case, the mutilation was inflicted by a person who had neither scientific nor anatomical knowledge." Bond suggested the police hunt for an ordinary, neatly dressed man who was middle-aged. He said a man of "great coolness and daring" committed the crimes.

While both profiles give police a certain type of person to look for, Jack the Ripper has not been caught.

This case fascinates me!

and couches. William Henry disappeared for a moment. He came back carrying a small tray of tea and biscuits, and we helped ourselves. Outside, the early evening sky had grown overcast, but I could still make out the midwestern prairie our train was traveling through. The flat landscape seemed to go on forever.

Setting my cup and saucer on a table, I went to a small chalkboard and wrote CRIMINAL PROFILE.

"Where do we begin?" Judge asked.

"If we are trying to track the criminal," I said, "I think it's important to look at the crime."

"It was a crime of poison," Judge said immediately, and I wrote CRIME IS POISON.

"Well," William Henry said, "to know something about poison, I would think you'd have to be educated."

"True," Judge agreed. While I didn't want to give the porter too much credit, I wrote EDUCATED on the chalkboard under CRIMINAL PROFILE. "What else?" I asked.

"You can poison someone from a distance," Judge said.

William Henry nodded. "Yes, it is not like using a gun or a knife, where you have to be near the victim. You can simply leave the poison somewhere, perhaps in food or drink. This could mean our suspect does not like to be around other people."

I wrote ANTISOCIAL on the board. But this seemed fairly obvious. After all, poisoning someone wasn't exactly a friendly thing to do.

"I have something I'd like to add," I said. I wrote the word ACCESS on the board. "Our criminal would have to have access to the scene of the crime. And I can only think of one person in this room who fits that description."

William Henry— MY prime suspect

William Henry's face turned dark.

"Now, now," Judge said, trying to cut through the tension again.

"Who else had the opportunity and the ability to enter the Pullman—"

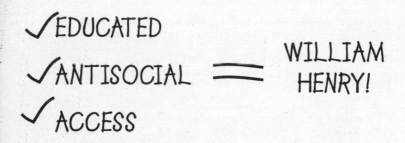

✓ EDUCATED

✓ ANTISOCIAL ═══ WILLIAM HENRY!

✓ ACCESS

"Enough!" William Henry suddenly shouted. And then as if catching himself, he said more quietly, "It's late. Miss Pinkerton has to take her leave and go to her bedroom."

"I will do no such thing," Justine cried. "We're making real progress here."

But William Henry wouldn't waver. He held up his pocket watch as if to show us it was time itself that made the demand.

However, he did cave in to one of Judge's wishes: I was allowed to sleep in one of the spare sleeping compartments. Thinking about the hard bench in the coach car, I eagerly accepted the invitation.

As I write this, I am basking in luxury in one of the Pinkertons' sleeping compartments. It's not very wide—I can almost touch the walls on either side at the same time if I stretch out my arms. But a person could sleep here happily every night. It has clean, fresh sheets over a mattress of soft down. Comfy, feather-stuffed pillows are heaped on top. And I have my own private bathroom!

Even in the middle of all this comfort, though, something is nagging at me. I can't help but wonder about William Henry. He had access to the government Pullman car, and he seems to match the description of our profile. Did he cut the investigation short because of his duty to Judge—or because I was getting too close to the truth?

This sure beats my wooden seat in the coach car!

I could get used to this!

This morning, I was once again awakened by the shouts of a girl—but now it was Judge, knocking loudly on my door. "Get up, Fitz! Meet me in the laboratory!"

I sat up in the amazing comfort of pillows and soft sheets. Why did rich people ever get out of bed? And I winced. Looking out the window, I saw the sun hadn't risen yet, and an orange-colored mist clung to the ground.

Getting myself together, I examined my appearance in the mirror to make sure I was the character I wanted to be that day. Then I headed out the door. The thought of solving the mystery of who poisoned Agent Howard added a little bounce to my step.

Judge's peacock pin

Judge was tapping her foot as I entered the laboratory. A purple pin in the shape of a peacock was shining on her gray blouse. "There's bread, strawberry jam, and orange juice on the table by the window," she said. "We can eat breakfast as we work."

As I helped myself to a piece of the delicious-smelling bread slathered with jam, she demanded impatiently, "What is our first task?"

I had to bite back a laugh. Judge might take it the wrong way if I told her that she reminded me of Teddy when he was waiting to sink his teeth into a bone.

I finished the toast quickly, wiped my hands on a napkin, and went to the work desk. I took the dollar bill I'd found on the platform from my pocket. "I want to find out who was in the government Pullman car around the time of the poisoning," I told Judge. "William Henry says only Agent Howard and he had access. But I think someone else was there."

"How do we prove that?" Judge asked.

"By comparing the fingerprint we got from the broken teacup to a print from the dollar bill I found in the station." As I spoke, I powdered the bill. "If the finger-prints from the teacup and the dollar bill don't match, that might mean there was more than one person in the government Pullman."

Normally, a bill would be covered with many prints as it passed from person to person. But this bill was crisp, as if it had not been in circulation for long. I found only two very good prints. One of them could be mine, I knew.

I lifted the two prints from the dollar bill. Then I placed the slide under the microscope next to the one containing the teacup fingerprint and began a step-by-step comparison.

The print from the teacup matched one of the prints from the dollar bill!

It's a match!

"What does it mean?" Judge asked.

I explained that the same person who held the teacup must have handled the dollar bill, too. That meant this person was one of

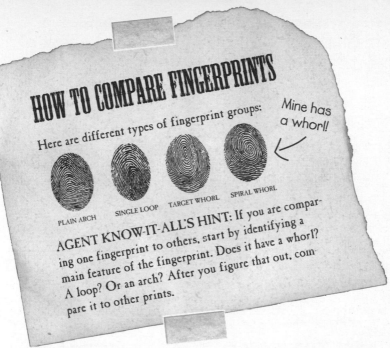

HOW TO COMPARE FINGERPRINTS

Here are different types of fingerprint groups:

Mine has a whorl!

PLAIN ARCH   SINGLE LOOP   TARGET WHORL   SPIRAL WHORL

AGENT KNOW-IT-ALL'S HINT: If you are comparing one fingerprint to others, start by identifying a main feature of the fingerprint. Does it have a whorl? A loop? Or an arch? After you figure that out, compare it to other prints.

the two people I saw boarding the government Pullman yesterday.

Judge didn't seem impressed. "But the prints probably belong to Agent Howard," she said. "He might have dropped the dollar bill that you found, and later, he could have picked up the teacup. That would mean that William Henry could still be correct; there was only one person on board the government car—Agent Howard."

"But you're making an assumption," I explained. "We don't know if the matching prints belong to Agent Howard. They might be someone else's. If we had a print from Agent Howard we could—"

"Dr. Freud won't let you near him," Judge said, shaking her head. "This morning I went to check on Agent

Howard. He's been moved to a compartment in the sleeping car. Dr. Freud wouldn't even let me look at him. He said the agent needed rest.

A good detective thinks fast. "There must be a way to get his fingerprint," I said. "I still believe that there was someone else in that Pullman—"

"Ayyyyyyyyyyy!"

A heart-stopping scream pierced the air.

"What in the world?" Judge asked, her eyes wide.

It was almost impossible to say where the scream had come from. But it had cut through the clanking of the train and made its way to the laboratory compartment of the Pinkerton Pullman.

"Nooooo!!!" Another scream, full of terror and anger, tore through the air. I felt cold fear squeeze my body.

"Someone needs our help," I said.

Judge gave a tiny nod. And with that, we rushed toward the door.

But before we could get there, it was thrown open by William Henry.

His eyes were wild. His shirttail had come untucked and stuck out of his pants. On anyone else this might not have been noticeable. Yet on a person who was always so in control of his appearance, it was unnerving.

Was William Henry the criminal after all? Had he come to attack us?

"Stay back," I said, starting to warn Judge.

That's when William Henry announced in a somewhat shaky voice, "I think another passenger has just been poisoned!"

Of course it's strange, but I was relieved in a way.

A poisoning meant the danger was outside the room, not standing right there with us.

"That's awful!" Judge shouted.

The three of us hurried from the room, heading toward the front of the train and the screams.

"Nooo! Ohhhh! My baaaaby! Help me, oh help me!"

The cries grew louder as we raced through the sleeper and the first-class car, where riders were looking at one another with confusion and fear.

When we ran into the coach car where my seat was located, I spotted Mrs. Notabe. She was sitting on the floor toward the front.

Still wearing her long black gloves, she cradled the limp body of her small daughter. Asyla's face was ashen. Her head was tilted back at an odd angle, and a line of spittle ran down her chin. Dr. Freud was kneeling over the little girl, one hand on her wrist to check her pulse.

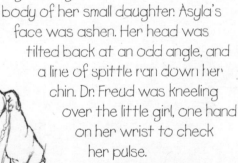

Asyla was out cold!

Judge, William Henry, and I stopped about three feet away, halted by the force of Mrs. Notabe's eyes, which flashed with rage. From this angle, I could see Asyla clearly. It seemed that William Henry had been correct about the poisoning. The little girl's fingernails and lips were a bright cherry red. I felt certain that if Mrs. Notabe had allowed me to get any closer, I would have smelled the odor of bitter almonds on Asyla's breath. But I knew if I moved closer, Mrs. Notabe would have scratched my eyes out, like a lioness defending her wounded cub.

Who on earth would poison a small child? It was now very clear that we were up against a ruthless criminal.

Dr. Freud stood up and turned to William Henry. "Bring me my bag at once. I must administer amyl nitrate to this child. In the meantime, we will give her fluids to—"

"You fool!" Mrs. Notabe hissed at him and pushed him back. "Get away from her! You would give fluids to the victim of cyanide poisoning? Is it your intention to kill my daughter? Get back!" Then turning her burning eyes on the rest of us, she shouted "All of you! I will care for my child!"

Just then Mr. Spike arrived. "What's this?" he asked, shocked at seeing the limp Asyla in her mother's arms. And then he quickly added in his syrupy voice, loud enough for the passengers to hear, "Seems someone else has a stomachache!"

Mr. Spike

Mrs. Notabe turned to Mr. Spike with her lips drawn back in a grimace. "If you take one more step in our direction—"

William Henry must have sensed that the situation might grow violent. He turned to us and said to Judge, "I want no arguments from you. Go to your dining car, and I will bring lunch to you."

Judge appeared tempted to argue, but she kept her mouth shut, and we both turned back toward the Pinkerton Pullman.

"Did you notice anything strange about all that, beyond the obvious, I mean?" I asked her as we walked through the first-class car.

"Yes." Judge nodded. "How did Mrs. Notabe know that her daughter had been poisoned by cyanide? That's something most people wouldn't know unless they have medical training."

"Or a detective background," I added. "I'll bet she knows more about Asyla's poisoning than she let on. I don't think she's being completely honest."

Judge glanced at me. "Well, she's not alone is she?"

"What do you mean?" I asked, confused.

"Someone else on this train is hiding something. And I'm not referring to the criminal," Judge said as we entered her family's dining compartment.

"What are you talking about?"

"Why, you, of course." Judge stopped walking and met my eyes.

"Me?"

"Yes, you," she said. "You are the liar. You're not a boy." She took a breath and continued. "You're a girl."

How did she know???

Before

After

- Hair under cap
- Attitude
- Posture

1:15 PM

My secret was out! But how did Judge

know? And what should I do? Deny it and keep up the act? My mind raced as I tried to decide.

It's strange. Revealing a secret about yourself can be like cracking a case. The secret can be something that you are unwilling to drag into the light. But there is always a sense of relief that the truth is finally revealed—no matter what the consequences.

Judge and I sat down at one of the mahogany tables in her family's dining compartment. Judge poured us cups of tea, then waited silently. I gazed out the window, watching the gray and brown landscape roll by under a cloudy spring sky as we entered the foothills of the Rocky Mountains of Colorado.

Finally, I decided to tell her my story.

"It's true, Judge. I'm a girl," I began, and then words poured out of me. "My name is Elizabeth Fitzpatrick Morgan. I was born and raised in London, England. My father is an inspector at Scotland Yard. It was his idea that I travel as a boy. In my country, our view of the United States is of thieving cowboys, acts of violence—"

"And cross-country trains full of poison," Judge added helpfully.

"Exactly." I nodded, grateful she was making this easy for me. "I know your country isn't all like that, but my father decided it's no place for a young lady to travel alone. He knows I enjoy disguises and want to be a

detective. Father couldn't come along on this vacation—
he's dealing with too many open cases. So taking this trip
in disguise seemed the perfect way to give me the things I
wanted most out of life—travel, excitement... and the
opportunity to go undercover."

Judge spoke softly. "My mother laughs when I tell her
that I want to go to law school. She says women are
supposed to stay at home. If it's good enough for her, it
should be good enough for me. Boys my age can run
around and play football, while I'm stuck learning to host
parties and sew. So I can understand your deception."
Here she paused and then asked, "But the story about
your brother. That's true, isn't it?"

"Yes," I said. "I wish it were part of my disguise,
but it isn't. I had an older brother. He moved to the United
States and joined the Navy. Later, he was killed on board
the MAINE."

Then I asked her, "When did you figure out my real
identity?"

"Almost the moment I laid eyes on you!" Judge
announced, grinning proudly.

"But how?" I had to admit I was upset that a nine-
year-old girl—no matter how wise—had seen through
my disguise.

Judge said, "If you'll remember, after you saved Agent
Howard, I pulled you back onto the train."

"Of course."

Her grin widened even more. "And my hand rested at
the base of your skull."

"Ah!" I realized how Judge had known that I was
not a boy.

I was betrayed by a small occiput bone! In a way I was relieved, it was something beyond my control that gave me away. "So it had nothing to do with my disguise or the way I talked?"

"No, you did an excellent job with both," Judge said. "But how were you able to change your voice?"

I told her about the three things I always keep in mind when disguising the way I talk.

SE YOUR HEAD!

he occiput, the knobby one at the base of the kull, is larger in males han in females. It is one way detectives can determine the gender of a skull.

THREE WAYS TO DISGUISE YOUR VOICE

You might not have time to study local accents before a mission. Beyond lowering and raising the pitch, there are other quick ways to disguise your voice:

1) End every sentence with a question mark. To see how this works, say "Go to the moon" and "Go to the moon?"

2) Place sturdy cotton pads on the inside of your cheeks.

3) Keep your teeth together while you speak.

"Wait a moment," I said, as something suddenly occurred to me. "Why did you wait so long to unmask me?"

Judge explained, "I knew you were in disguise but I didn't know why. It could have been for some evil purpose. I never really thought you were the villain, but it wasn't until Asyla Notabe was poisoned that I could be a hundred percent sure."

Now I understood. "Because we had spent the morning together," I said.

"And I knew you didn't have time to slip off and poison Asyla," Judge finished my sentence. She stuck out her hand and I shook it. "Nice to meet you, Elizabeth," she said.

"And you, Judge," I said. "It's a relief to have someone know the truth. But please continue to call me Fitz. I like the nickname, and I promised my father that I'd travel in disguise. I want to keep my promise."

Judge nodded. "I think we'd all like a disguise at this point. Just in case you've forgotten, someone has poisoned two people on this train!"

Glad to turn back to the case, I said, "Actually, we only know that two people have been poisoned on this train. We don't know if the same person is responsible. There may be more than one criminal! We need to focus. Do you have paper and a pencil?"

Judge fetched them and poised the pencil over the paper. "What are we writing?"

"A list of our main suspects. First on the list, I think we should put—"

List of Suspects:

1.

2.

3.

Just then William Henry entered. He set down two plates of steamy, rich-smelling beef stew and two cups of fresh tea. "Asyla Notabe is going to be fine. Dr. Freud doesn't think her dose of poison was as strong as Agent Howard's. She's already out of her coma. In fact, she keeps complaining that she wants to play a game in the baggage compartment."

"Hide-and-seek?" I asked.

"Yes," William Henry said, surprised. "How did you know?"

Judge spoke up. "What about her mother? Did Mrs. Notabe say anything?"

"Funny you should ask . . ." William Henry's sentence trailed off.

"What's funny?" I asked.

"Asyla's mother now seems to accept Mr. Spike's explanation of a stomachache. Yet, she herself thought Asyla was poisoned at first." William Henry noticed the paper and pen. "And what are you two plotting?"

"We were just coming up with names of suspects."

"Were you now?" William Henry said, not really listening. He flicked open his pocket watch and checked the time. "I'm off to the mail car, if you need me. The pole that picks up the mailbags from along the side of the track is acting up. Mailbags are flying into the mail car faster than greased lightning. One man was hit by a bag and it snapped his wrist!"

Judge asked, "Why don't they just stop using it?"

"The train's got to pick up the mailbags—no matter how dangerous it is! Folks in San Francisco are expecting to get their letters and packages," William Henry said as if the answer to Judge's question was obvious. And with that, he left the compartment.

Turning back to our suspect list, I said, "I'm definitely writing his name here."

Judge's eyes grew wide. "You don't mean to put William Henry on the list?"

I nodded firmly. "And not just anywhere on the list. At the top."

"Oh, I don't know," she said doubtfully.

"Think about it." I leaned toward her. "His uniform is all shiny and buttoned up. Everything must be by the book. That pocket watch seems to run his life—"

"He works on a train!" Judge protested. "Schedules are the most important things to workers on the train."

"Someone that tightly wound is bound to snap. You can tell by looking at his hands! They're stained with grease—"

"Because he loves to tinker with machinery!"

There was no stopping me, and I continued, "And he's got those long arms and legs. And what about those blue eyes of his?"

too-blue eyes

pocket watch always in hand

greasy hands

spotless uniform

Judge gave me a long look. Then a smile flashed across her face as if she were just starting to understand something. "All right, I'm willing to consider him as a suspect. But you have to admit, he is rather nice looking. I wonder if you're being totally objective."

"I don't know what you mean," I said, gazing at my hands. When she didn't say anything, I continued, "All I know is, he matches the profile. He's educated, and I find him very antisocial. Plus, he had access to the government Pullman. He could easily have served Agent Howard the poison in food or tea."

A second passed, and then at the same time, Judge and I reached out to push our teacups away.

But before my fingers touched my cup, I had a sudden thought and asked Judge, "Can you get your evidence kit?"

She returned a moment later with it, and using the fingerprint equipment, we lifted one of William Henry's fingerprints from the teacup.

Placing the slide back in its case, I said, "We can compare this print to the one on Agent Howard's cup. That might show whether William Henry touched the agent's cup at some point."

"Good idea, Fitz. Let's get to the lab to check them under the microscope," Judge said. We got up from the table and left the dining compartment.

Teddy was waiting for us when we walked into the laboratory. He sat on the dark blue rug, his tail wagging furiously, as if he were terribly proud of himself. Something furry with a tail of its own dangled from his mouth.

"Oh no!" cried Judge on spotting this. "The poor kitty!"

My determined little dog had found what I had sent

him searching for yesterday: the cat. But the creature in his mouth was lifeless.

Judge shook her head sadly. "This is too much."

I plucked the cat from Teddy's mouth, scratched between his ears, and told him, "Good boy! I'll get you a special treat from the dining car later." He wagged his tail a bit more, plopped down on the ground, and was soon snoring.

Refusing to look at the cat and shocked by my behavior, Judge started to ask, "What on earth are you doing?"

I gave the cat's head a sharp twist.

"Ahhh!" Judge yelled.

The cat's head popped right off.

"Not to worry. As soon as I took the cat from Teddy, I knew it wasn't a real cat. But it is a clever way to conceal secrets." I showed her

What a good boy!

how the fur was just a covering for a hard hollow cylinder.

Reaching into the cat-shaped container, I pulled out a small envelope. Written on it in dark ink were the words: USS MAINE Evidence.

Staring at the word Maine, I felt a familiar sadness as an image of my brother came into my mind. Judge seemed to be reading my thoughts. "Fitz, what could all this possibly have to do with the MAINE? Why would Agent Howard hide something inside a cat?"

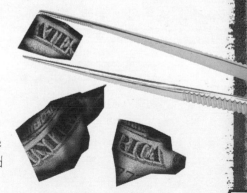

I snapped back to the business at hand. Inside the envelope were pieces of singed paper. I could see the letters "Uni" and "ate," the date 1895, and other numbers and squiggly lines.

"I don't think this is ordinary paper," I said, heading to the microscope.

"What do you mean?" Judge asked. She watched over my shoulder as I placed the pieces of paper under the magnifying lens. Then, using tweezers, I began to move the pieces around.

It was clear the burned bits of paper were from a five dollar bill. But that fact was not what made my heart skip a beat.

"Aha!" I cried. I stepped back from the table. I had just cracked at least part of the case!

Before going any further, I took a second to consider all the evidence. And then my mind made the connection!

I explained my discovery: "Look at the serial number on this bill. It has the same number as the dollar bill I found in the station."

"But that can't be," Judge shook her head. "Each bill has its own unique serial number. The number shows where it was made and what printing plate was used. The one dollar bill and the five dollar bill cannot have identical serial numbers."

"But these two do," I said. "Take a look."

The serial number

Judge leaned over the bills to examine them. Her expression went from doubt to shock. Her eyes met mine. "The numbers are exactly the same!"

I nodded. "There is only one explanation."

"At least one of these bills is a fake!" Judge cried. She turned to the bookshelf and removed a magazine

IS MY CASH TRASH?
How to Detect Counterfeit Money

Counterfeiters usually find out that creating fake paper money is not as simple as it sounds. There are many security measures working against them, including . . .

1. **Design:** The pictures and borders on paper currency are complicated for a reason—the more complex the design, the harder it is to copy.

2. **Ink:** The green in U.S. "greenbacks" has a very unique look. Counterfeiters have attempted to re-create this green color using everything from cyanide-based dyes to fruit juices. But it is very difficult to come close to the true color.

3. **Paper:** High-quality, very expensive material that gives paper bills a certain feel.

Glad I tore this out of DETECTIVE'S MONTHLY

entitled DETECTIVE'S MONTHLY. There was an article inside called "Is My Cash Trash? How to Detect Counterfeit Money." She handed it to me. "This should help."

Poison! Counterfeit currency! I had wished for mystery and adventure. And it had come—**in trainloads!**

Greetings from the Rockies!

The landscape actually did look like a postcard!

April 16, 1906
6:00 AM

Why should the start of my fourth day
on the train be different from the others? It began, of course, with someone shouting.

I had just opened my eyes after a restless night's sleep. Even the Pinkertons' deep feather pillows couldn't stop me from having nightmares of faceless villains and pools of steaming poison.

I had left the window curtain open, thinking the starry sky might lull me to sleep. Now the window let in the cool gray light of a cloudy dawn. A forward jerk of the train let me know the locomotive was struggling up a rather steep incline. We must still be in the hills around the Rockies.

"It's only six in the morning; try to go back to sleep," I told myself. I was sinking back into the lemon-scented covers when a shouting voice rang outside my door.

I leaped from the bed, dressed hurriedly in my disguise, and flung open the door. I was just in time to see the porter heading down the hallway calling, "Telegram! Telegram for Miss Pinkerton!"

And, as I sat down to begin writing, I spotted a strange piece of paper poking slightly out of my journal. When I slid the paper out, I found a note.

DO NOT GET INVOLVED!
THIS WILL BE YOUR
ONLY WARNING!

It could only be from the poisoner! Or at least that made the most sense. But how did he or she manage to slip the note into my journal? The only time it's out of my sight is while I'm bathing or sleeping. The thought that the person who is poisoning people on this train might have been in my compartment while I slept sends chills down my body.

With trembling hands, I checked to make sure my compartment door was locked. I sat down on my bed and flipped through every page of my journal—but there were no other messages.

Who left me such a frightening note? And how did that person get it into my journal?

Once again, my suspicions turned to William Henry. He probably has a key to my room, and it'd be easy for him to sneak in and out.

To prevent any more tampering, I'll keep my journal with me at all times.

Was it William Henry?

6:30 AM

When I recovered from my shock, I went to Judge's compartment and pounded on the door. Finally, she opened it and glared at me sleepily. "First the porter with a telegram from my parents and now you. I think the real mystery is why no one wants me to sleep—"

"Judge, listen!" I interrupted her. "I've got a piece of shattering news."

Her eyes went wide, and I could see I had her attention. She said, "Let me grab us some breakfast, and I'll meet you in the lab."

Fifteen minutes later, we had each finished a slice of bread and jam, and Judge was pacing the carpeted floor of the laboratory. I had just told her about the note in my journal. Her surprise was almost as great as mine.

After a moment, she asked, "Are there any fingerprints on the note?"

I shook my head. "While I was waiting for you, I checked the note for prints. The sender must have been careful because I could only find my own."

"Why would someone leave a message in your journal?" Judge tapped her chin thoughtfully. "Why not just slip it under your door?"

"I don't know," I answered. Then an idea came to me. "I found the note in the middle of an entry I had made yesterday. Maybe it was left in that spot for a reason."

"What was the entry about?" Judge asked.

"It was right after you told me how you knew I was a

girl," I said. "We had started to make a list of suspects when William Henry came in. He told us about Asyla feeling better and that she wanted to play a game in the baggage compartment."

"Right!" Judge agreed. "And then he said something about Asyla's mother, didn't he?"

We both stopped pacing and looked at each other.

"Yes," I said, feeling that we might be on to something. "William Henry told us it was strange that Mrs. Notabe had accepted Mr. Spike's explanation that Asyla had a stomachache. Especially after she had said Asyla was poisoned."

Hmmm ... Would Mrs. Notabe break into my compartment and leave me a warning note because I was writing about her daughter? That seemed unlikely.

Judge and I talked about it a while longer and realized that we weren't getting anywhere.

Finally, she sighed and collapsed into a chair. "We seem to be stuck. We just keep coming up with questions and no answers!" Judge's voice was filled with frustration. We need to focus, I thought.

"Let's write down our questions and see which ones we can answer," I said, picking up a new piece of chalk.

MY QUESTIONS

- Main question: Who is poisoning people?

- Why are people being poisoned?

- Is the MAINE part of the puzzle?

We stared at the board. Finally I said, "Okay. I have two questions we can answer," and wrote them down. Then we took turns writing down possible answers.

WHO ARE OUR SUSPECTS?

- William Henry Moorie
- Mrs. Rabella Notabe

WHAT ARE OUR CLUES?

- broken teacup with fingerprint
- dollar bill with fingerprint, possibly counterfeit, from station platform
- singed remains of bill from fake cat
- note left in journal
- Agent Howard and Asyla Notabe both victims of poisoning

"We might be able to upgrade one of these two from suspect to criminal," I said, pointing to the list of names. "And we have the clues to do it."

"How—?" Judge started to ask, and then answered her own question. "The fingerprints!"

We went to work.

I began comparing William Henry's print to the one I had found on the broken teacup.

"Well . . . ," I said, pulling back from the microscope and rubbing my eyes.

"Well what!" Judge yelled impatiently. "Is there a match?"

"Unfortunately, or I guess fortunately for William Henry, there's no match," I told her.

"What does that mean?" Judge asked.

No match

"We cannot directly link William Henry to the crime. But we can't take him off the list either."

Judge thought for a moment. "And we can only say this about one of our suspects."

I agreed. "Yes. We don't have a fingerprint from Mrs. Notabe."

"I'm not sure she is such a strong suspect," Judge said. "Would she really poison her own daughter?"

I remembered the way Mrs. Notabe had screamed in panic while holding Asyla. "She did seem very upset about Asyla's poisoning. So I'd say the answer is no. She didn't poison Asyla. But that doesn't mean she didn't poison Agent Howard."

"There's only one thing to be done," Judge said. "We need to get Mrs. Notabe's fingerprints to rule her out."

"Or link her to the crime," I added. "But she wears those long gloves all the time. Did you notice she didn't even take them off when she was holding Asyla after she'd just been poisoned?"

Even as I was talking, a plan was taking shape in my brain.

"There might be a way," I said, eyeing Agent Howard's fishing line. "But we'll have to be crafty."

"Which is right up your alley," said Judge with a grin.

What a pair!

The sun has set over the horizon,

transforming the clouds into bright shades of purple. This beauty seems to be lost on most of the passengers, though. They are not feeling lively. One thing I now know about train travel is that, after four nights, the endless rocking, the constant shrieking of machinery, and the smell of food that's no longer fresh all can take a serious toll on passengers.

Most of them had closed themselves up in their compartments or sat dozing in their seats.

I took all this in as Judge and I paused before stepping into the first-class car. I looked at the girl next to me. She had dark hair and thick, heavy eyebrows. Blocky heels added nearly three inches to her height. The only splash of color came from the purple beaded necklace she was wearing.

"My name is Maximillion Millions," I told her. "And yours is Henrietta Gotgobs."

Judge looked back at me through lids heavy with rich eye shadow, and her mouth seemed to twist under the weight of the lipstick.

"Exxxcellent!" she said in a long, drawn out, snooty manner, and I had to control a laugh.

Wearing makeup and clothes one of her cousins had left on the Pinkerton Pullman, over her own clothes, Judge looked and spoke like a different person. I hoped I looked just as impressive, wearing the old brown suit jacket and black top hat we had found in a closet. If things went wrong with my plan, I didn't want Mrs. Notabe to know we were involved.

"Are you ready, Henrietta, for Operation Coin Grab?" I asked Judge, giving my voice a southern twang.

"Yes, dahling Maximillion," she responded in her snobby accent. "It's time we make 'cents' of this mystery."

We opened the door to the first-class car and started down the aisle. According to William Henry, Mr. Spike had moved the Notabes to this car after Asyla was stricken.

Our investigation had been stalled since yesterday morning. For Operation Coin Grab to work, the first-class hallway had to be free of other passengers and porters—and that meant we had to wait for the right moment.

As we passed the Notabes' compartment, I saw that the door was open a crack. I took a quick look inside. Mrs. Notabe sat in her seat, reading a book. Asyla was curled up asleep on the bench next to her.

As planned, I said loudly, "Aren't you carrying the jeweled purse with the hole in the bottom?"

"Why, no!" Judge responded, playing the part of Henrietta Gotgobs perfectly. "This jeweled purse was repaired by one of the maids."

Then I tossed a five-cent coin attached to a piece of fishing line to the floor, making sure that the coin banged loudly off the door of the Notabes' compartment. It clattered to the hallway floor.

Leaving the coin in place, Judge and I continued down the hall. At the end of the car, we crouched against a wall to see if Mrs. Notable took the bait.

For a long moment nothing happened. I was afraid our mission had failed. But then a hand wearing a black glove appeared through the doorway of the Notabes' compartment. The gloved fingers found the coin, but the tiny bit of glue we had used on it made the coin hard to move. The fingers tried sliding the coin back toward the compartment, but it would not budge. Finally, the hand disappeared back through the doorway. Seconds later it was back, but this time it was not wearing the glove.

I KNEW she'd fall for it!

I heard Judge take in a quiet breath of anticipation. Wait... wait... I told myself, thinking of my father who told me patience is as important as a hook when it comes to fishing. "Want to end up with air for dinner?" he'd say. "Then just forget to pack your patience when you go fishing."

As Judge and I watched, the bare hand tried to pick up the coin, but the fingers only brushed along the coin's surface.

Come on! I wanted to shout.

Finally, the index finger of the hand shot out—and we had what we had come for. The finger had pressed down firmly onto the coin, giving it a solid fingerprint.

Yes! I imagined the fish closing its mouth around the hook. I yanked on the fishing line that was attached to the coin. The coin jerked—and the hand suddenly smacked down on it, trying to keep it in place.

I pulled again, but still the coin was held by the weight of the hand.

This was not part of the plan! Judge and I should have been long gone by now with the fingerprint sample safely in our grasp.

Framed by long black hair, Rabella Notabe's perfectly made-up face suddenly appeared around the corner of the compartment door. Keeping her hand firmly on the coin, she leaned toward it.

As she moved her finger so that she could pick up the coin, I pulled the fishing line with all my might. The coin flew from under her hand and shot toward us. I reached up and caught it in midair in my own gloved hand.

There was no time to celebrate. Mrs. Notabe raised her head and made eye contact with me. For one instant, she gave me a creepy smile like a panther spotting its prey—and then she let out a shrill scream.

Instantly, doors opened and faces popped out of compartments. Judge and I were turning to flee when Mrs. Notabe screamed to a porter, "Those two thieves stole from me!"

No! I wanted to shout. That's not true!

But Judge and I panicked, and we didn't stay to hear any more.

We had to get away as fast as we could. I could hear Judge's feet pounding after me as we raced out of the car, with people shouting at us to stop. If we could just find a hiding place and remove our disguises, we'd be safe.

Through the coach car, the dining car—where startled passengers looked up from their roast beef dinners—we raced toward the front of the train. The car that housed the train employees was next—and we dodged around some workers who were sitting at a table playing cards and some who were folding sheets at another.

We were running out of train cars! If we didn't find someplace to remove our disguises soon,

The dining car

we would reach the locomotive, the end of the line for us.

Finally, we reached the mail car. Basically, it's a mobile post office. One wall is taken up with row after row of slots where mail is sorted. Usually, three or four men are there, sorting the mail that's been picked up along the route. But it was deserted now.

The other wall has a long sliding door that was open to the cool night air. The door allows workers to reach down into the net that catches the mailbags left for pick-up along the side of the tracks.

For some reason, William Henry's face popped in my head as we entered the car. It wasn't a completely unpleasant image. But I also heard his voice, and that was more upsetting.

"Mailbags are flying into the mail car faster than greased lightning. One man was hit by a bag and it snapped his wrist!"

We shouldn't be in here.

"Judge! Wait!" I cried.

But I was too late.

Judge was two steps ahead of me. As she started to turn toward me, the train jerked, and there was a strange grinding sound.

The amazing thing is that the train does not have to stop in order to pick up or deliver bags of mail to different areas of the country.

Bags for pick-up are left on poles along the tracks. A steel frame supporting a net is extended from the side of the train. When the train passes by the mailbags, the net scoops up the bags and carries them off. To drop off a mailbag, the opposite procedure is followed. A bag is extended from the train by a steel pole, and nets along the tracks catch them.

Suddenly a 10-pound mailbag flew in from outside. The brown canvas bag knocked squarely into Judge and sent her sprawling. The system was still malfunctioning!

Look out, Judge!

As I rushed toward her, I heard the grinding sound again. Out of the corner of my eye, I saw a blur rushing at me. I barely had time to throw myself backward before a mailbag rocketed between Judge and me. The net that is supposed to hold onto the mailbags until a worker reaches in to retrieve them wasn't doing its job. Instead, it was acting like a giant slingshot, plucking the mailbags off poles and firing them into the car.

Judge and I looked at each other from across the car. Judge appeared winded and confused. She rubbed her side where the bag had hit her, but she looked unhurt. Then she was on her feet, running for the other end of the car. "Come on!" she called back to me as she ran from the mail car toward the baggage car.

But I wasn't going anywhere. As another mailbag fired into the train, I realized I would be a fool to follow her. One of those bags could kill me.

I took off the top hat and jacket, pulled my cap out of my pocket, and put it back on, then turned to face the music.

The door from the workers' car slid open. The train officials, led by Mr. Spike, rushed into the mail car.

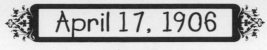
Without a word, William Henry walked

me to the storage closet in the dining car. He opened the door and waved me in. The closet's shelves were jammed with tablecloths, napkins, canisters filled with wooden spoons—all the day-to-day things needed for the dining car to run smoothly.

There was barely room inside for the two of us, and William Henry's clean, soapy smell filled the closet. He watched my eyes traveling over items on the shelves and said, "We don't keep any sharp objects in here, if that's what you're looking for."

Who did he think I was? He was one of the suspects. I wasn't!

I opened my mouth to defend myself, but he cut me off. "Mr. Spike ordered me to keep you in a safe location—"

"And do you always follow orders?" I snapped.

"When they make sense, yes, I do," William Henry shot back. "Stealing from poor Mrs. Notabe at a time like this, with her daughter just getting well. What were you thinking?"

I couldn't help wincing at his words, which were filled with disappointment. "Mrs. Notabe isn't as innocent as she appears."

"And how about you?" William Henry's eyes finally met mine and he studied me. "Are you all that you appear?"

Now it was my turn to look down. Did he know I was a girl? The pots and pans made a strange tinny song as the rocking train banged them together. It seemed pointless to explain who I really was. If he was the poisoner, nothing I said would matter. And if he wasn't, the truth about my identity would just add to his suspicions that I was up to no good.

Taking my silence as an admission of some kind of guilt, William Henry said, "That's what I thought. Now I have to finish the task Mr. Spike gave me. Not to worry, I won't have this job for long. Once the Pinkertons discover that I've lost their daughter on board this train, I'll lose this job faster than you can say 'balloon juice.'" He started to leave the closet.

"Wait! William Henry, listen to me." I had to do something; I had to stop him! "I think we're in danger. Everyone on this train is at risk!"

"Yes, from children with too much freedom. But that's about to be solved as well."

"You can't lock me in here!" I said, shocked.

"You're right," he said. My panic eased, but returned when he added, "There's no lock on the door. So I'll have to find another way." With that William Henry took a screwdriver from the long pocket of his jacket and started to remove several screws from the doorknob. "You know why I like machines so much?" he said. "There's a sense of order to them. You turn a switch and you know the light will come on. You twist a screw and you know a bolt will tighten. But people, that's a different matter."

I didn't know what to say.

The doorknobs on both sides of the door loosened, and William Henry slid both of them out of the sockets and into his pocket.

He was leaving. Do something! I shouted at myself.
"William Henry," I said. "Before you go, promise me one
thing. Go to the Pinkerton Pullman. Look at the list of
evidence we have on the chalkboard—"

He just shook his head and cut me off. "We'll let your
family sort this out. Now I've got to track down your
accomplice, Miss Pinkerton."

He closed the door, and I was left alone in the dark.
The only light was the circular glow from the empty hole
in the door, where the doorknobs used to be.

I have to get out of here! I told myself. But how? Then
I remembered something I'd learned from my father and
got to work.

SURVIVAL GUIDE
for
EVERYDAY LIVING

Imagine your door is closed. You
reach to open it and the doorknob is
gone. Somehow, it fell off and disappeared. You have a tricky
problem on your hands. But do not panic! The rod or spindle that
is attached to the doorknob has a rectangular shape for a reason. Its
edges turn the cam that constricts the spring and pulls back the
latch. This opens the door.

However, you do not have a spindle, so you will need to make
or find one of your own!

I found a butter knife and used its dull edge
to whittle a wooden spoon into the shape of
a spindle. It took me a long time!

The door to the Pinkerton Pullman opened with a loud click, and for once, I was happy for the deafening noise of the moving train. I had used my detective skills to escape from the storage closet and managed to sneak down the length of the train without being spotted.

I had been hoping to find Judge in her family's car, but she wasn't there. The car's windows framed the darkness of the outside. Without Judge there, the clacking sounds of the train echoed around the empty compartments like lonely ghosts. It made the car seem like a mobile haunted house.

I knew that I had limited time before my escape was discovered, so I rushed to the laboratory. A wave of worry for Judge hit me. If she was in danger, one of the ways I could help her was to figure out who the villain was. So I set to work. I carefully took the coin Mrs. Notabe touched from my jacket pocket. After lifting her fingerprint, I compared it with the broken teacup fingerprint under the microscope.

The fingerprints did not match!

This fact didn't prove she was innocent. But it didn't link her to the crime of poisoning Agent Howard either.

So? I thought. Who's left? We're running out of suspects! I went to the chalkboard to see if I could come up with a new plan.

I was so intent on the task that I didn't hear someone coming up behind me.

A shaking hand fell on my shoulder.

Dropping the chalk, I wheeled around and nearly screamed.

The cry died in my throat as I recognized the person standing in front of me. It was Judge.

"Oh, it's you," I started to say, and then I felt like screaming again. It was Judge, but her hair was disheveled and her eyes were rolling about in her head.

Her cherry red lips suddenly parted and her voice emerged like the squeaks of an amateur violinist. "I cracked the case," she wheezed. "I figured it out—"

Then her legs buckled and she began to sink to the floor.

Oh, no! Not Judge, too!

My worst fear had come true!

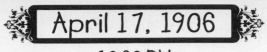
Somehow I caught Judge and gently

lowered her to the floor. Her face was close to mine. There was no denying the smell of bitter almonds that came with each gasping breath.

"Judge! Judge!" I cried, but knew that she could not hear me. She was unconscious.

I took her wrist and felt her pulse. Quick and shallow. Her nails shone as red as her lips.

Judge had been poisoned!

I was able to lift her, and I carried her to the living quarters. I laid her on the sofa where just days ago we had placed Agent Howard. I eased her head carefully onto a pillow.

Her chest rose and fell quickly as she took short, ragged breaths.

I had to get help! Something had to be done and fast. If Judge didn't receive an injection of amyl nitrate to counteract the cyanide in the next thirty minutes, she might die.

"You're going to be all right," I whispered to her, patting one of her cold hands, which had clenched into a rigid fist. I was turning to leave when I noticed the edges of a piece of paper poking out from between her fingers.

Was this paper what Judge had found to make her think she had solved the case?

I reached for her hand and began prying her fingers open—**Wham! Wham! Wham!**

There was a heavy pounding on the compartment door between the living quarters and the laboratory. I froze, thankful that Judge must have locked the door after she entered.

Wham! Wham! WHAM!

Thoughts of the paper in Judge's hand flew out of my head as muffled shouts came from the other side of the door. The train officials must have discovered my escape and tracked me to the Pinkerton car!

That was good news for Judge. They would be able to help her. But who would help me? I wondered. Mr. Spike would lock me up. William Henry was a suspect. And the poisoner was still on the loose!

Who could I trust? No one on the train, except for Judge—and she was even more helpless than I. I needed to contact someone. Anyone would do, as long he or she was not on this train. But how?

Then it hit me—of course! I rushed to the window.

When trains break down or fall behind schedule, the train crew has to have a way to call for help. Otherwise, trains coming from behind or in the opposite direction might crash into them. I knew that the owners of the Continental Express had set up a telegraph system that runs along the entire length of the track between New York City and San Francisco. A series of telegraph boxes—one every

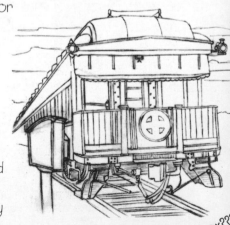

Where's the nearest box???

few miles—taps into this system and allows people to communicate over hundreds of miles.

I had to reach one of those boxes and telegraph for help!

But how? The train was racing along at more than thirty miles per hour. I couldn't just leap off the side.

There was one way....

I didn't give myself a chance to consider the consequences. I moved quickly to the back of the car.

"Hold on!" I shouted, hoping the men outside the door would brace themselves.

And then I pulled the emergency brake.

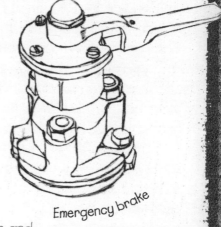

Emergency brake

The results were immediate and terrifying. The train screamed as if in agony. Books, glass vials, pictures, and all sorts of small objects flew off shelves and smashed into walls. I was thrown off my feet and across the compartment as the brakes sank their teeth into the wheels, slowing the train to a halt. I looked up, battered, but not severely hurt. Judge had rolled over but remained on the plush couch.

"Help will be here in a moment, Judge," I told her, even though I knew she couldn't hear me. "I'm going to let the outside world know we're in trouble."

I ran out the rear door and onto the connecting platform between the Pinkerton and the government Pullmans. Leaping over the side, I tumbled down a grassy slope. Then I was racing away from the train, searching desperately for a telegraph box.

The moon seemed to follow me, casting a sinister light that flickered as it passed through puffs of clouds. I couldn't shake the feeling that something other than the moon was pursuing me.

As I sprinted along the track, I stole glances to my left at the lonely, dark landscape. The only signs of life were several tall trees whose twisted branches stood out against the night sky.

My foot slipped on some loose rocks and I nearly stumbled. But I kept my balance and continued rushing headlong through the darkness. Relax, I told myself, trying to calm down. It won't do Judge or yourself any good if you trip and break your leg.

I had only been running for a short time when I spotted a rectangular shape the size of a small medicine cabinet. Bolted to a pole about four feet from the ground was a telegraph box!

It was locked!

If I had time, I would have hugged the wooden box. But my excitement was quickly deflated. The box was locked. No! I wanted to wail. I've come too far to be stopped by some lock that probably cost only a few pennies.

I looked around for a large rock. When I finally found one, I hefted it into the air and, with one swift motion, brought it down on the lock. The lock stayed put, but the hook it was attached to snapped in two. The lock fell to the ground, and the door of the box swung open.

I breathed a sigh of relief and imagined I could hear Judge say, "Bully for you!"

You never know when Morse Code will come in handy!

The telegraph device itself was easy enough to use. Just press down on the metal transmitter bar and send out the message.

I started to telegraph my call for help:

> Continental Express in trouble. Stop.
> Dangerous criminal on board. Stop. Alert
> authorities. Stop. Current location is

That's as far as I got when I heard—**Snap!**

I looked up and cried out in frustration. The wire that was used to connect the telegraph box to the line above was now blowing loose in the breeze, hitting the back of the box with a mocking sound.

I'd been tapping out a message to no one.

A feeling of dread suddenly gripped me. I knew I had to find another telegraph box. And that meant I had to stumble farther away from the train into the darkness.

I gazed back toward the train with longing. It remained at a standstill about a hundred yards away. Warm squares of light spilled from its windows, making it appear as friendly and inviting as hot chocolate on a snowy day. But looks can be deceiving, I reminded myself.

Toughen up, Fitz, and get moving.

That train sure looked good!

Before I could do anything, though, the moon emerged from behind the clouds and cast my shadow on the rocky ground along the tracks.

I gasped.

Next to mine there was another shadow. Someone was right behind me!

I bit back the urge to scream and slowly turned around.

Out of the darkness emerged a pale face. A face with

a strange birthmark under the right eye. A mark rather like the shape of Asia.

I rubbed my eyes, thinking the vision would disappear, but the figure remained. It was Killian.

My brother!

He was reaching one hand out to me.

It can't be you! You're dead! I wanted to shout. But my tongue was frozen.

My head swam. I felt my knees give way. And then I fainted.

This is what I must have looked like all tied up!

When I woke up, I was on the train.

The side of my head ached. It took me a minute to focus my thoughts. Of course. I must have hit my head on the ground when I fainted. I tried to rub it, but I couldn't.

I was sitting in a chair in the Pinkerton's laboratory, about two feet away from the door to the compartment. My arms and legs were tied with rope. There was a knot at my wrists, one at my ankles, and two more holding my back and lower legs to the chair.

The train rocked. We were moving again.

I opened my mouth to call for help, but then I thought better of it. What if the person who had tied me up was in the next compartment? Shouting out would alert him or her that I was awake.

The rope bit into my skin, and the knots tightened as I struggled against them.

Above it all, a thought pounded rhythmically in my head like a driving piston: Killian is alive! Killian is alive!

It had not been a dream. I had seen him. But what was he doing on this train?

And Judge! Where was she? Was she safe?

If I was going to answer any of these questions, I had to escape these ropes! With as much energy as I could muster, I arched my back, pushing up and away from the back of the chair. But the rope refused to give.

Then I remembered my detective training: The more you struggle, the more the knots will tighten!

Thank goodness I kept this tip!

YOUR "KNOT HERE" GUIDE

A square knot will tighten when tension is put on it. It can be untied, however, by grasping both sides of the knot and pulling them apart.

A slipknot grows smaller under strain, but can usually be untied by pulling one end.

My eyes ran over the knots holding me captive. They looked like square knots. I desperately hoped I was right. If I started pulling on the wrong part of a knot, I could make matters worse.

Slowly I worked my hands back and forth, sliding the knot that held them up so it rested on my forearms. This freed my hands slightly, and my fingers were able to reach the knot. I was tempted to move quickly but knew jerking motions might only tighten the knot more.

"Don't panic," I told myself. "You have to take your time."

Click.

I heard the sound of a key entering the lock on the other side of the door. My eyes went to the brass doorknob.

My body's instincts screamed for me to thrash even harder against the ropes. But I forced myself to stay calm.

Focus your thoughts! Slow movement is the only way!

I heard the key turning in the lock. The doorknob started to turn—steady, steady.

I used my fingers to pull on one side of the knot, and my teeth to pull on the other. The square knot untied. My hands slipped free! I started untying the knots that held my legs in place—

The door opened—just as I managed to climb to my feet, feeling woozy as the blood rushed to my head and darkened my vision. When my sight cleared a second later, I went into my defensive stance.

I was looking at the grim face of one of the top suspects. It was William Henry!

Madame Esme's
ACADEMY OF SELF-DEFENSE

If your assailant is facing you and swinging with the right hand, take this defensive stance:

1. Feet pointing forward with right foot at a 45 degree angle from left.

2. Left leg bent at knee, right leg straight.

3. Plant feet firmly for a strong base.

4. Keep eyes open and on your opponent..

5. Swing your upper body backward, forward, or side-to-side to avoid oncoming blows.

6. If a blow cannot be avoided, block it by sweeping your right arm out and up.

Self-defense is about being prepared

But when he opened his mouth to speak, he didn't let out an evil laugh like some criminal mastermind. Instead, he said, "You're awake. Thank goodness."

He sounded honestly glad to see that I was okay. Fine, he was not the poisoner. But I had a feeling he was the one who bound me to the chair.

"How dare you tie me up!" I shouted at him.

William Henry held out his long arms in an apologetic gesture. "We found you on the floor. You were unconscious. You stopped this train—illegally, I might add—and probably tampered with the telegraph system—once again, illegally. The train officials demanded that you be bound to the chair so you couldn't do any more mischief. It was either that or put you back in the storage room." Seeing my rage, he added, "I am sorry. Truly."

"Where's Judge?" I asked, unwilling to forgive him. He stared at me blankly. "Justine! Where is Miss Pinkerton?"

"With Dr. Freud and Teddy. She is out of danger and asleep. She survived both the cyanide and the amyl nitrate. . . . " William Henry's voice trailed off. My cap must have fallen off when I fainted, and I could see his eyes

William Henry seemed different!

finally taking in my long brown hair. The wheels of his brain turned, and then he said: "Hey! You're a girl!!"

I rolled my eyes. "Good detective work, inspector," I said sarcastically. "Where are we?"

William Henry appeared slightly stunned that I wasn't a boy. He replied, "On a train."

"I know that." I assumed my natural English accent. "But where is the train?"

"Just about to pull into San Francisco. Because of you, we're arriving late. It's 4:45 AM."

I had thrown the train off schedule. In his mind, this was apparently one of the worst things a person could do.

He looked at me closely. "Who are you? Are you British?"

We didn't have time for this. I said, "Let's make a bargain. I'll explain everything to you later, and you can ask your questions then. In the meantime—"

"We have a few other issues to deal with," he said, finishing my sentence.

"Exactly. For instance, where is Agent Howard?"

"He's gone. I can only guess that he came out of his coma. But he's nowhere to be found! We're afraid he might have fallen off the side of the train."

"I must speak with Judge right away," I demanded.

William Henry shook his head. "As I said, she's safe but asleep. Dr. Freud doesn't want anyone to disturb her."

I was about to insist that we see Judge when William Henry said, "She was holding this when we found her. The only words she said before going to sleep were 'Give it to Fitz.'"

He handed me a crumpled dollar bill. This must be what

Judge had in her hand when she collapsed. I looked at it more closely. It had the same serial number as the bill I'd caught on the platform and the one I had reconstructed.

"Was she repaying a debt?" William Henry said.

"No," I answered, remembering the way Judge had saved my life by pulling me back onto the train. "I'm the one who is in her debt."

"Then what does the bill mean?" he asked. "Why was it so important that you get it?"

"Good questions," I admitted. I thought back. The last time I had seen Judge before she was poisoned, she had just recovered from being struck by the mailbag and was running toward the front of the train, toward the baggage car.

Suddenly, this memory was replaced by the image of a little girl with pigtails tied in blood-red ribbon whining for me to wake up so that I could play with her in the baggage car.

The journal entry where the note had been left was about . . . the baggage car.

"Of course!" I shouted. "We have to get to the baggage car!"

I started toward the door, but William Henry stepped in front of me. "Look. I've just discovered that you're not an American boy but an English girl. For all I know, you could be the poisoner. If you want me to let you go, you have to convince me there's a good reason." He pulled out his pocket watch and flipped it open. "You have thirty seconds, and then I'm going to tie you up again." It was clear that he meant what he said.

I spoke quickly. "All right. I know it sounds crazy, but here's what I think. Someone is smuggling counterfeit money to San Francisco. The money is in the baggage car."

"Balloon juice," he said. "How do you know that?"

"Because at least two of the three people who were poisoned had gone into the baggage car."

"What are you talking about?"

"Both Judge and Asyla were in the baggage car at some point. Don't you see? The dye used to make phony money contains cyanide. The money must have been printed recently, and some bills were still wet. I think Agent Howard was investigating the counterfeit money. That's what the Secret Service does. I'll bet he touched the wet bills, and his skin absorbed the cyanide dye."

"So you're saying he accidentally poisoned himself?" William Henry nodded, thinking it over. "But what about Asyla Notabe and Miss Pinkerton?"

"Simple," I replied. "Asyla played in the baggage car and must have snooped in a bag holding the money. Judge must have discovered the bills when she was hiding there from the train officials. Everyone who comes in contact with large quantities of the fake money is poisoned. We have to hurry. Once we pull into San Francisco, the suspects will leave the train. They'll be gone—"

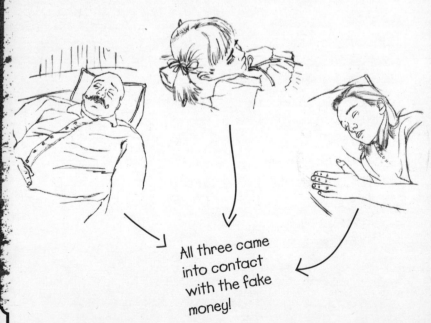

All three came into contact with the fake money!

"What suspects?" William Henry interrupted me. "If the poisonings were accidental as you say ... then there are no suspects."

"Of course there are!" I cried. "You're forgetting about the counterfeit money. Someone is smuggling it on board this train. And if we don't get to the baggage car before we reach San Francisco, we'll never catch the criminal. You have to make a decision now, William Henry. There's no time!"

William Henry gazed down at the watch in his hands. Doubt clouded his features as if he were asking himself, What if this timepiece doesn't have all the answers?

After a moment, he snapped the watch closed and tucked it into his pocket.

He nodded at me and said with a lopsided grin, "Well, whoever you are, what are we waiting for? Let's get to the baggage car!"

William Henry looking at his pocket watch—again!

Welcome to San Francisco!

And what a trip it's been!

5:00 AM

If someone reads this journal in the

future, they'll discover a guide on what to do if he or she is riding on a train full of poisoned passengers and counterfeit money. But as William Henry and I raced toward the baggage car, no such guide existed—and I realized that even with all my training, nothing could truly prepare me for this unique and dangerous situation.

"Wait," I whispered, and William Henry stopped just as he was about to open the door to the baggage car. "We can't just barge in there. We don't know who or what we'll find inside."

"So what do we do?" William Henry asked.

At that instant the train began to shriek in an eardrum-bursting way. It was braking. We were pulling into the station in San Francisco. We were almost out of time!

"What should we do?" I wondered out loud.

"Either we go in now or we'll be too late," a voice said from behind us.

Startled, I turned around to discover—

"Judge!" I cried—instantly glad the sound of the brakes covered my shout. I threw my arms around her.

I had missed my friend more than

Thank heavens!

I realized. We hugged tightly. Then questions flew from my mouth. "Are you all right? What are you doing here? Shouldn't you be in bed?"

She laughed at my excitement. "You're here, so I guess William Henry gave you my message."

"You're an amazing detective, Judge. That dollar bill you gave him led us here." I then took a good look at her. She was very pale, but her lips had lost their frightening bright red color.

Before I could ask any more questions, she said, "Not to worry, Fitz. I feel like I've been run over by a train, but I'll be okay. When I woke up, Dr. Freud was in a chair by my bed and Teddy was at my feet—both snoring. So I crept out of the compartment."

"You . . . " William Henry spoke for the first time since Judge's arrival. I prepared myself for his long list of reasons why Judge should return to the safety of her Pullman.

Judge didn't rant or rave as she once might have. She simply looked into his eyes and said quietly, "William Henry, I have to be here. This is my case, too."

"You . . . " he repeated, but something about her manner seemed to have changed his tone. "You're right on time. You have no idea how much I admire that," William Henry said, using almost the same words as when they had first met.

Judge's grin widened. "Well, now that that's settled, we have a mystery to solve."

I nodded, and the three of turned back to the baggage car door. Using the deafening sound of the brakes as cover, I opened the door a crack and peered inside.

I had only seen Agent Howard in a semiconscious state and later in a coma, so it was strange to see him standing in the center of the luggage- and crate-filled room. Like Judge, he looked tired. His clothes were rumpled and his handlebar mustache drooped slightly, but otherwise, he appeared fit. Even odder was the group of five people who surrounded him.

What a difference!

Each of them wore black hoods that covered their heads and faces. They held bills and they were looking at them through one of the three lenses that were attached to their hoods.

I took in all this in half a second. I was about to cry out and warn Agent Howard that he was in danger. People do not wear hoods unless they are trying to hide something. But just as I was about to shout, "Stay away from him," the agent spoke, and his words shocked me into silence.

THIS THING REALLY SPOOKS ME!

A hood like this is used by secret societies. There are three different kinds of lenses on the hood. They slide over the eye sockets to reveal or block out secret information. The hood's function led to the term "hoodwinked"—still used today to describe when the truth is kept from someone.

"Remember to keep your gloves on at all times while handling the bills. The ink should be dry now, but it's better not to take chances—I speak from experience."

No! A voice cried in my head. Agent Howard was working against the law!

He tapped his foot impatiently and shouted above the shrieking brakes of the train, "Well, what do you think? We have to move along quickly. This car will be flooded with porters retrieving luggage for passengers in no time!"

The hooded figures began nodding their heads, and I could hear them saying "Excellent work" and "Genius."

"How do we know you won't fail us again?" a female voice said from within one of the hoods. "We don't want another incident like the MAINE."

"Right," another of the hooded figures chimed in. "Howard, you assured us the explosives from that ship would be used to destroy the central bank in Cuba—and that the counterfeit money would easily replace real money in the confusion."

"We've gone through this already!" Agent Howard said. "It's not my fault the explosives meant to carry out our plan destroyed MAINE. It was an accident. Things will be different when you destroy the bank here in San Francisco." He looked at his pocket watch anxiously. "All that's left is for you to pay me for forging millions of dollars for you."

As I watched through the crack in the door, a hooded figure stepped forward. A few long, black hairs had escaped from under the hood. Handing Agent Howard a suitcase, she said, "Your payment is inside this case."

Counterfeit money???

Agent Howard's face broke into a triumphant grin. "At last!" he said. His hand touched the handle of the suitcase— and suddenly the baggage car was a blur of activity! One of the hooded figures tore off his mask. I gasped. It was my brother, Killian! No! Is he one of the bad guys, too?

As if to answer that question, Killian rushed forward and slapped handcuffs on Agent Howard, shouting, "You are all under arrest!"

In a flash, the long outside doors of the baggage car were rolled open. A spooky, yellow glow from the electric light over the large station clock cast long shadows of the people approaching on the platform.

"Federal agents! Don't move!" A swarm of men jumped on board the train, holding up badges and guns.

Without thinking, I opened the door all the way. William Henry, Judge, and I took a few steps into the baggage car, drawn to the action like moths to a flame. Men were pushing and shoving, agents were tearing the hoods off the figures.

"Mr. Spike?" William Henry said as the bald head of his boss emerged from one of the hoods. Mr. Spike! I thought. That's why he didn't want to launch a real investigation. He's one of the criminals!

Agents were leading two handcuffed men out the large side door and off the train. But wait! Where was the hooded woman?

Mr. Spike was a criminal!

My eyes scanned the back of the room. I spotted her moving among the shadows, making her way to a position behind my brother. From the way she was slinking, I knew she was preparing to attack him.

I took a step forward. William Henry grabbed me, trying to hold me back. I yelled, "Killian! Watch out!"

For a moment, time seemed to stand still. Killian's head swiveled, and he stared at me in utter surprise ... The hooded woman behind him froze ... The other agents stopped ... Outside there was a **kerdunk!** as the station clock clicked over to 5:13 AM....

And then I began to shake. *No!* I thought. *No! I can't faint again ... not now!* But I realized it wasn't just my body that was shaking. The entire baggage car was rocking. Outside the open doors, people on the platform were thrown around as if they were rag dolls.

It was an earthquake!

Even though the earth beneath us rolled and heaved like a stormy ocean, the woman kept her feet. She ran swiftly toward the baggage car door. My brother spun to stop her but lost his balance and fell.

The woman zigzagged, passing within feet of us as she sprinted to the door. Judge darted forward and caught the back of the woman's hood, ripping it off her head. The woman shoved her, and Judge was thrown back against the wall. William Henry rushed to her side.

I gaped at the person Judge had unveiled. It was Rabella Notabe.

She dashed to the wide doorway and paused there for a moment. She screamed above the chaos, "You'll be sorry for this! Each and every one of you!" But she was looking only at Judge and me. Then she jumped out the wide door and disappeared into the darkness.

Not as steady on his feet, Agent Howard started to follow her out the door.

"Oh no, you don't!" I said.

My next act might not reflect my training as an expert detective, but it was quite effective.

I stuck out my foot.

Agent Howard tripped. Once again, I managed to keep him from leaving the train. He tumbled, hit his head, and collapsed unconscious into a corner.

I couldn't believe it!

The earthquake raged on.

Awful tearing sounds exploded around us. The track buckled and sent the baggage car tilting to the side. Outside, the wooden structures of the station simply collapsed into themselves like houses made of toothpicks. Two agents huddled by their prisoners, and a third stumbled over to Agent Howard to handcuff him.

Wham!

A telegraph pole snapped and tumbled on top of the train with so much force that it crushed part of the baggage car. The roof over Killian caved in, and he disappeared from view.

"Killian!" I screamed. William Henry rushed over and tried to hold me back, but I ran into the dust-filled darkness. To find my brother and lose him again in one day was more than I could stand!

"Elizabeth," I heard Killian answer, calling me by my real name.

I followed his voice and found him buried among the scattered bags and wreckage. His legs were trapped under a massive trunk and heavy, jagged pieces of the roof. Even at this awkward angle, we managed to hug.

My brother!

"What a sight you are, Elizabeth..." His voice trailed off in a hoarse whisper. Tears streamed down his cheeks.

"You're alive!" I hugged him again.

Suddenly, finally, as if someone had turned off a switch, there was silence.

The earthquake was over. For now. I knew there could be aftershocks just as deadly as the quake itself.

The intense quiet quickly filled with the moaning of injured men and women and the groaning of structures that were in danger of collapsing. William Henry and Judge made their way over to us, and we began working to free my brother from the debris.

"But, Killian, what are you doing here?" I asked, hoping to distract him from the pain of his injured legs.

"Yes, Elizabeth," he said. "I owe you an explanation, even though it is against the rules.

"I work for the United States Secret Service," he continued. "Our main mission is to crack this counterfeit ring. We called it the Calamity Crew. The Crew created disasters—like explosions. Then, while authorities were busy dealing with the disaster, the Crew switched real money with counterfeit bills."

I couldn't keep the "you're crazy" tone out of my voice. "Are you telling me the Calamity Crew planned this earthquake?"

Killian choked back a little sob. Then he continued. "No, this earthquake wasn't part of their plan. But the Crew would have used the confusion that follows to switch the money."

To keep his mind off the pain, I said, "And what about Nathan Howard? Was he a real Secret Service agent?"

At the mention of the name, Killian's face darkened. "Sort of. Howard and I both worked on this case all these years. We were stationed together on the USS MAINE. But 'agent' was just his cover. Howard was actually part of the Calamity Crew." He sighed heavily. "Eight years ago, he smuggled explosives on board the MAINE. He was going to blow up Cuba's national bank. In the confusion, it would have been easy for the Crew to slip counterfeit money into use. Unfortunately for everyone, Agent

Four members of the Calamity Crew!

USS MAINE SINKS!

At 9:40 PM on February 15, 1898, this great ship blew up and sank in Cuba's Havana harbor.

Howard did not know much about explosives. The MAINE exploded and sank."

William Henry rubbed sweat from his eyes with the back of his sleeve. "Then why didn't you arrest him sooner?"

"I couldn't prove it until now," my brother answered. "I had to catch him in the act."

I thought of all the pain my family had gone through. "Killian, why didn't you just tell Father and me that you were alive?"

"I wanted to, more than you can know. I'm sorry," he said, and I saw tears in his eyes. "President Roosevelt himself instructed me not to tell anyone that I was investigating the USS MAINE. Eight years. It's a long time to be undercover, but these are dangerous criminals. The sinking of the MAINE led to a war. The president urged me to see the mission through. Once this case was solved, I was going to contact you and father. And that day came sooner than I planned, thanks to you—"

Killian winced as William Henry lifted a large piece of the roof off his leg. "So you were on the train this whole time." I needed to keep him distracted.

"You're a good detective, Elizabeth, but I recognized you through your disguise the first night on the train," my brother said. "I was walking through the coach car to stash the 'cat' in a safe place—and spotted you."

"That was your cat?" Judge asked between grunts as she attempted to heave the trunk to the side.

"Yes," Killian answered. "I kept evidence that I didn't want Agent Howard to find in that container. It makes a good hiding place. After I saw you, Elizabeth, I knew I had to hide or you might blow my cover!"

The pieces started coming together. "So those were your fingerprints on the teacup?"

Killian nodded. "I was in the government Pullman while you were saving Agent Howard. I didn't realize he was in danger. I heard shouts coming from the platform. In my rush to help, I dropped the teacup. But by the time I ran outside, you'd already rescued him. After you and the Pinkerton girl dragged him into the living area, I made my way quietly through the Pinkertons' hallway. I've been hiding on the train ever since."

So it was Killian who broke the threads, the alarm devices, in Judge's hallway!

"Then you stayed in hiding except . . . " I knew the answer, but I wanted to hear it from him.

He finished my sentence. "Except when I delivered that note." He must have seen something flash in my eyes. "I know the message I left you about not getting involved must have terrified you, but that was the point. I wanted you to be too scared to keep snooping. I wanted to keep you out of danger."

We lifted another jagged bit of debris off his lower body, and my brother was nearly free. "But why did you put the note in that journal entry?" I asked.

"I picked the lock to your compartment, Elizabeth, and planned to leave you the warning note. Then I remembered what a wonderful detective you were. Another set of eyes—especially keen ones—could really help my case, I thought. So I read your journal. I had just started reading the entry about the baggage car when

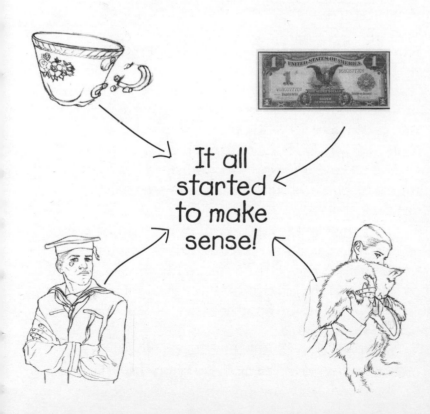

It all started to make sense!

you stirred in your sleep. Thinking you were about to wake up, I slid the message into the journal and ran."

Killian's face broke into a grin. "So, I'm sorry I read your journal, but I'm also glad! What you wrote about the baggage car made me think. I realized that's where the fake money must be hidden. If I waited here in the baggage car long enough, the Calamity Crew would show up to get the counterfeit cash. Then I could nab them. Thanks to that entry—thanks to you," Killian gave my shoulder a squeeze, "we cracked this case."

His eyes locked with mine. "I wanted you to be safe and not get involved in this case. I didn't think it was proper for a girl. But you did, and I'm very grateful. You helped solve an eight-year-old mystery!"

My cheeks flushed from the praise. Judge smiled at my embarrassment. "Bully for you!"

"You deserve as much of the credit as I do," I said to her.

"It's true," Killian said. "From what I saw in Elizabeth's journal, you played a vital part in the case."

Now it was Judge's turn to blush.

One nagging question remained. "But why did you cut the telegraph line when I was trying to send out that message?"

"I didn't! After I saw you jump off the train, I followed you to protect you. I didn't cut the line. It must have snapped on its own. After you fainted, I carried you back onto the train and left you in the Pinkerton Pullman."

Finally, we freed my brother's legs. He was in pain, but nothing was broken.

William Henry and I supported him on either side. We helped him climb down out of the baggage car and onto the platform. Killian spoke briefly to agents. He instructed them to take Mr. Spike, Agent Howard, and the other captured members of the Calamity Crew to a safe spot on the platform. When things calmed down, they would be hauled off to jail.

Above us, the sky was a frightening orange. San Francisco was on fire.

For a moment, William Henry, Judge, my brother, and I stood next to the train. Killian and I grinned at each other in the middle of all the madness and chaos. I didn't know what to say. My brother was alive! I couldn't wait to telegraph Father!

Then William Henry urged us forward. "Come on," he said. "Let's see what we can do to help."

The burning city was a terrible sight!

The four of us walked back toward the passenger cars. Everyone's hair and clothes were sweaty and smudged with dirt. People were running about. Panic seemed to be growing around us.

About a hundred yards ahead, I could see Dr. Freud near the side of the tracks. Carrying his medical bag, he moved among groups of passengers and train crew, checking on their condition.

Dr. Freud happened to look our way. Even from this distance, I could see the relief on his face when he spotted Judge. I waved to him and mouthed the words, "We did it!" I don't know if he understood exactly what I meant, but he smiled broadly and turned back to the passengers.

"There's Teddy!" Judge said, pointing to a spot near where Dr. Freud worked. My heart leapt when I saw my dear dog. A little boy and an older woman were sitting with Teddy on the edge of the platform. The boy's arms were wrapped around Teddy's neck.

Teddy sat with the boy patiently, comforting him. Suddenly, my dog's nose pointed up in the air. His big head swiveled and he looked at me, his tail wagging furiously as he made a little hop.

He smiled at me!

Before he could come bounding toward me, I quickly made three flicks with my index finger and put my palm to my heart, telling him in Teddyspeak, STAY and GOOD BOY.

136

It was best for him to stay out of danger and comfort the little boy. We would be reunited soon enough.

As the four of us walked, my brother took my hand. I held his with all my might. "Killian, do you know what it's like to meet someone that you know you will be friends with forever?"

Killian said he did. Judge put a hand on my shoulder, knowing I was talking about her.

Teddy was safe. Good boy!

I continued, "Well, imagine my surprise. I've met two people like that on board this train—even if one of them is full of balloon juice."

Despite the dim light, I saw William Henry blush and look away with a smile. His perfectly clean uniform was a thing of the past. After our adventure in the baggage car, his hair and clothes were smudged with dirt and sweat. But he looked good, even like that.

Two men walked quickly toward us, their eyes darting here and there. One was carrying a large camera and the other made notes on a pad of paper. Clearly, they were journalists.

"What will we call this disaster in the newspaper?" one of the men asked the other as they approached us.

Without thinking I said, "The Big One."

Judge looked at me, surprised.

The journalist who had asked the question overheard me. I saw him write down what I had said.

"The Big One," he repeated as he passed by us. "Yes, I think that will work."

Breaking news!

<u>WARNING</u>: This letter reveals the story's ending!

A NOTE FROM THE AUTHOR

SWINDLED! takes place in the past, but that doesn't make it a history book. While I tried to be accurate when it came to the detective techniques of 1906, I wrote this book to be entertaining. So, when historical events weren't what I needed them to be—presto! I changed them for the sake of the story.

Fitz, Judge, the train itself—all seem very real to me and, hopefully, to you. But they are inventions of my imagination. The book's biggest example of "historical fiction" is the made-up cause of the USS MAINE's destruction.

There's no doubt that the MAINE sank in Cuba's Havana harbor in 1898 and that this event sparked the Spanish-American War. Many historians say the most likely cause was a mine that bumped up against the MAINE and exploded —but, to this day, no one is completely sure what really happened.

I thought it would make the adventure more exciting if Fitz helped solve one of our country's oldest mysteries—so I created the Calamity Crew.

I hope you had fun reading SWINDLED! Just don't use Fitz's journal as study material for your next history test!

Yours in time,

Bill Doyle

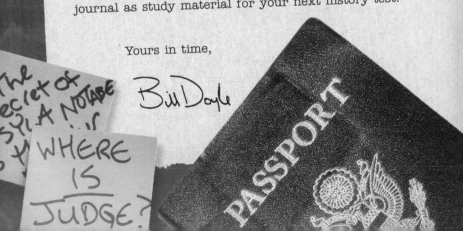

The secret of SPI-A NOTABE is

WHERE IS JUDGE?

ABOUT THE AUTHOR

Bill Doyle was born in Lansing, Michigan, and wrote his first mystery when he was eight. He loved seeing the shock on people's faces when they discovered the identity of the story's villain—and knew then that he was hooked on writing. Bill has written for Sesame Workshop, LeapFrog, Scholastic, ROLLING STONE, TIME FOR KIDS, and the Museum of Natural History. He lives in New York City with a mysterious dachshund named Esme.

Check out these other gripping Crime Through Time™ books!

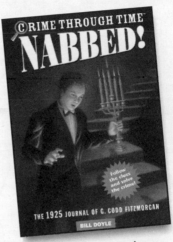

Now in stores!

Now in stores!

Now in stores!

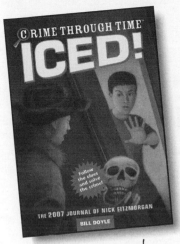

Now in stores!

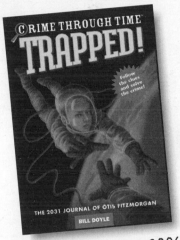

Coming in November 2006!

EXTRA! EXTRA!
Don't forget to read the newspaper in the
back of each book!

THE INSPECTOR

5¢   **We Have an "EYE" for News**

"THE BIG ONE"
STRIKES SAN FRANCISCO!

EARTHQUAKE AND FIRE LEAVES CITY IN RUINS

SAN FRANCISCO (AP)—A massive 30-second-long earthquake struck San Francisco at 5:13 AM on April 18, 1906. This powerful quake and its aftershocks destroyed much of the city. Broken gas lines helped feed a raging fire that burned for four days, reducing the center of San Francisco to ashes. More than 1,000 people lost their lives.

WILL DREYFUS GO FREE?

PARIS—It's been twelve years since French army captain Alfred Dreyfus was convicted of treason for spying. Today, thanks to handwriting comparison and other detective work, he might be cleared of all wrongdoing.

TRAIN ROBBERS STEAL STATION!

Yes, there are now hundreds of miles of track running across this great land of ours, but the trains that run along them do not interest a certain group of mysterious figures. About a year ago, they stole an entire station building from the Central Railroad of New Jersey and no trace has been found. Recently, yet another building was erected— and has disappeared just as mysteriously!

PEOPLE

KELLER SPEAKS OUT

At a recent rally, Helen Keller demanded rights for those less fortunate. In 1882, an illness struck Miss Keller, making her deaf and blind before the age of two. Alexander Graham Bell, the inventor of the telephone, also taught the deaf, and he introduced Annie Sullivan to Miss Keller. Miss Sullivan became Miss Keller's teacher, lifelong friend, and interpreter while she attended college. Miss Keller graduated from Radcliffe in 1904, and has become a leader in the fight for the rights of the disabled.

PEACE OF MIND

Lawyer Mohandas K. Gandhi began a campaign of non-violent resistance to protest the treatment of Indians in South Africa.

DREAM IN FLIGHT

What's next from the two brothers who brought us the first powered airplane flight in 1903? Orville and Wilbur Wright are working on a plane that can stay in the air for half an hour and fly figure eights!

FOOD

NEW COCA-COLA

Prompted by threats of legal action, the Coca-Cola Company replaced the drug cocaine in its drink with the stimulant caffeine.

MISTAKE OR FLAKE

BATTLE CREEK, Mich.—This year, W. K. Kellogg opened the Battle Creek Toasted Corn Flake Company. Toasted cereal flakes were an accidental invention at the health spa run by W. K.'s brother, J. H. Kellogg. Word has it the two brothers are no longer speaking because J. H. doesn't approve of W. K.'s adding sugar to the product.

OOKS

Sir Arthur Conan Doyle has written *Sir Nigel*—too bad Doyle's best creation, Sherlock Holmes, doesn't appear in the book!

Reading Upton Sinclair's *The Jungle* may make you lose your lunch, but *The New York Times* called this exposé of Chicago's meatpacking industry "brilliant."

Mark Twain's latest story, "The $30,000 Bequest," oozes with the charm and humor that are the trademarks of the author of *Tom Sawyer*.

ASK DR. NOITALL

"What should one do if trapped in the wilderness with nothing but a telegraph device and an empty canteen?"

You will be glad that you live in these modern times. Just this year, the distress signal SAVE OUR SOULS, or SOS for short, has been introduced. SOS was chosen because it is easy to tap out in Morse code (just three dots, three dashes, and three dots). Tap it out, take a seat on your canteen, and wait for help.

ASHION

FOR THE LADIES ...
Want to look like a well-to-do lady? Then be sure to cover everything but your face and hands! Don that long skirt, pull that corset tight around your waist, and pile that hair on top of your head!

FOR THE GENTLEMEN ...
Men who want to dress down can leave the top hats at home. A brown business suit and tie is good for just about any occasion. But don't forget your soft felt or straw hat!

CLASSIFIED SECTION

Traveling to San Francisco?
Check into a first-class hotel in the center of the city!
Hotel Salmona
Rates: $1.50 per day
Special attention given to investigators!

. . . .

Photographs for Undercover Agents
Vincent, Allegan & Co.
Mott Street, New York City
Phone East 756

Honest Values in Detective Disguises
Men's Wigs $2.00
Elevating Shoes $1.35
Nurse Uniforms $2.25
Schoenfeld's on Southfield
Detroit, Michigan

. . . .

Automobiles
RAMBLER Model 15,
4-cylinder vertical motor,
35-40 H.P. $2,500
REO Runabout $700
M. S. Busque & Company
223 Deming Street
Chicago, Illinois

SPORTS

FULL OF BALLOON JUICE?

LONDON—American Frank Lahm won the world's first international balloon race. Lahm flew 402.4 miles from Paris, France, to Flying Dales, England, beating out fifteen competitors from six different countries.

WORLD SERIES PREDICTIONS

CHICAGO—Our sports reporter in the field predicts that teams from the same city will take part in the third World Series. According to his prediction, the Chicago White Sox of the American League will do battle with the Chicago Cubs of the National League.

ENTERTAINMENT

DO NOT PANIC!

When you go to the movie theater to see the very first animated film, remember that the rolling eyes and the cigar smoke are cartoons—not real. Recently when people visited the nickelodeons to see *The Great Train Robbery,* many thought the bullets were real. Well, just as no bullets were flying off the screen then, no eyes will roll into the audience now. So stay seated and enjoy the show.

THANKS, TEDDY!

WASHINGTON, D.C.—Good news for nature lovers! President Theodore Roosevelt—the rugged outdoorsman who inspired a toymaker to create the teddy bear— is currently inspiring campers and sightseers across the country. On June 8, he will sign the National Monuments Act to establish the first 18 National Monuments, including the Grand Canyon!

BANDS IN A BOX

NEW YORK—The Automatic Entertainer is here! The first jukebox that lets you preselect what you want to hear is now being produced in the United States.

SCIENCE

BLOODY GENIUSES

Add Clemens von Parquet to the list of Austrians who have transformed the world! This year, he introduced the term *allergy* to describe the physical reaction (which can range from sneezing to death) caused by different substances that only affect certain people. Parquet joins Karl Landsteiner, who discovered each person has one of at least three different blood types: A, B, or O, and Dr. Sigmund Freud, who invented psychoanalysis.

HOW NOBEL!

Marie Curie, the first woman to a win Nobel Prize, was spotted at a recent dinner in honor of physicist Albert Einstein's 27th birthday on March 14

....